To Chris
With best wishes

Sarah

THE RIVER WOMAN

SORREL PITTS

Indigo Dreams Publishing

First Edition: The River Woman

First published in Great Britain in 2011 by:
Indigo Dreams Publishing Ltd
132 Hinckley Road
Stoney Stanton
Leics
LE9 4LN

www.indigodreams.co.uk

ISBN 978-1-907401-57-2

British Library Cataloguing in Publication Data. A CIP record for
this book can be obtained from the British Library

Designed and typeset in Minion Pro by Indigo Dreams

Cover image by Irene Lamprakou/Trevillion Images

Printed and bound in Great Britain by Imprint Academic, Exeter

*Papers used by Indigo Dreams are recyclable products made from
wood grown in sustainable forests following the guidance of the
Forest Stewardship Council*

'Until she strides in again beyond her shadows
And cancels everything behind her.'

Seamus Heaney

Acknowledgements

First and foremost to my agent, Tara Wynne at Curtis Brown, for keeping the faith, and to all at Indigo Dreams for turning the dream into reality.

To my family for their encouragement and patience. And to Sarah Moncrieff and family, Tibet Kara, Murray Cooper, Deborah Heron, Boyanna Elks, Nicky Wicks and Kevin Leahy for always being there. Thanks too, to Emily Rosser, Deirdre Gyenes and Barbara Mercer for the loan of their talent and professionalism.

Special thanks go to Sir Michael Parkinson for promising me an honest opinion – thank goodness it was a good one!

And finally, thanks to Mike Scott, musician and poet, whose genius has inspired me throughout my life.

For my father, Denis Pitts

THE RIVER WOMAN

PART ONE

Chapter One

I have to make a decision.

I know that I'm not in the best frame of mind for this. For a start, I'm nearly dead from cold, and in a near-death state it's hard to think clearly about the simplest of things. But in my case oncoming death has brought a strange kind of clarity. It has done away with all those confusing shades of grey and left me with a very simple dilemma. That dilemma is whether to live or to die.

I am only thirty years old. But I have done something very bad. No, that is a euphemism. I have done something terrible: something which I know I deserve to die for; something which I have planned to die for.

Here is my death scene. It is the middle of winter. I am sitting in the snow on an old bridge in a big field somewhere in Wiltshire. My bare legs hang over heavy blocks of sharp-edged sarsen stone which rise, in a rugged curve, over a wide stream. I stare into its depths, absorbed by the endless sifting of flint and weed. Freezing snow cuts into the crook of my knees and my feet dangle over the swollen, ice-grey waters.

I have been sitting here for hours, since early morning, and believe me the cold, when it gets you, hurts like nothing else. So many pains .... I'm confused, but I concentrate on the water and the frightening fact that soon I'll be completely numb.

The snow, glittering and virgin, covers the river banks and forms sad moustaches on the naked branches of trees. A blackbird's song drifts over its silver slopes. The large, now familiar, house on the distant hillside frowns at me, no doubt wondering what on earth I'm doing on such a day, in such clothes, wishing to die. In my mind I picture its inhabitants, sitting beside a fire, the rosy glow on cheeks, a newspaper, mugs of sweet tea. They are oblivious to this girl who has followed them all day in her tortured imaginings.

I raise my gaze from the water and look at the house longingly. It is perhaps a mile away, the only human structure on the bleakest of landscapes. The house is the reason for my change of heart. I do have not much time left. My story may end here, forever untold, or it may begin without a history, without an explanation. These are critical moments.

But as my body begins to pull itself back from the water's edge, I see I have already made my decision. My spirit, that house, fear – I'm not sure what, is propelling me away from the death's edge, the abyss. I know I can do nothing but cause further pain, I know my way is littered with crumpled motivations, inexcusable curiosities, petty logics. Although I'm crazy, believe me, I'm quite sane. I know what I'm doing, I just can't stop it. It's because I need answers. I thought that this would be an answer, this frozen end, serenaded by the gentle song of the river. Evidently it's not.

It seems to me that there's more reason in my living than in my dying.

I lever myself away from the bridge and begin to crawl, my knees and hands pushing into the deep snow, slow, hesitant, pausing every few feet. Then, forward again, a death-shadow over my shoulder and the waters beside me. I am cold, so cold, my body hurting, every inch a victory, every twist of a limb a signal to my blood to keep moving, keep flowing.

I force myself to straighten, but movement has already brought back some circulation and my body is losing its stiffness. I wobble, pressing a hand into the snow, and rise to my feet. The water drifts, and from the mauve taint coating the suffocating winter sky, I see that evening is approaching. With evening more snow will come.

I am dizzy but I can stand. And walk. Every part of me aches but I can walk, slowly at first, my breath on the air, my arms gripping my stomach. It's more a lurch than a walk, but those old-men trees by the field's edge begin to look not so distant, and the river's voice is growing silent.

I do not know how long I struggle before I see him. I clamber through a barbed wire fence, gashing my hands and legs, though I can barely feel the pain for the cold. I'm in a second field, the large house is as distant as ever and now the light is fading. I realise that, like a desert, the landscape obscures distance – what seems like half a mile may be five miles, what seems like twenty minutes may be twenty days. All I know is that the dying of the light is the dying of my spirit. Weakness returns. It is the end of the day. I let my body sink back into the snow. Of course it is not fair for me to live.

And now I really hate myself for this double betrayal – deciding to live, only to die. I will look such a fool to them all, such a callous fool. They will find me here tomorrow, my death spread on the snow, my arms outstretched, blue, bloodied, my mouth and eyes open, gazing at hell.

And they will know what I have done.

I open my mouth to pray. But then I see him and the prayer unfolds into a long breath of relief. He's hurrying from the direction of the house, his wild hair falling around his face as he pulls his long legs through the drifts. Our eyes meet for a second before mine fall.

'Help me.'

Thirty seconds, a minute, and I feel him kneel beside me, a hand on my shoulder.

'Help me.'

He's speaking to me but I cannot hear what he says. I don't

care. I only know that his voice is as soft as the snow – it sounds like warm honey pouring over a silence as cold as the ground beneath me.

I raise my head with a painful jerk and, with the briefest of glances, take in as much as I can of the stranger. He's looking down at me through a tangle of brown curls, his wide, youthful mouth pursed, his eyes large and afraid.

He kneels and takes off his jacket. 'Here,' he whispers.

He places the jacket carefully around my shoulders and produces a small bottle from its pocket. He twists off the top before pushing the cold glass to my lips. I splutter and cough and the liquid runs over my cheeks and neck.

'Drink it.' He puts a hand under my chin and forces my head up, pouring the whisky down my throat as one would give medicine to an unwilling dog. It sears my stomach like a hot sword cutting through ice. A thin wail escapes into the silent, late afternoon air as I fall into firm arms which lift me upwards.

'I'm going to get you home.'

I shake my head, forcing an arm against him and pushing his body from mine. But the cold has left me weaker than a child. He pulls me forward and my head lolls against him.

'No, let me rest. Please, let me rest.'

'There's no time. My father is a doctor. He'll take care of you.'

My balance fails and I stagger against him. He pulls my arm over his shoulders. I cannot lift my head and stare blindly at the white snow under our feet. He half-lifts, half-drags me through the drifts.

'What's your name?'

I shake my head.

The snow sucks us down. I feel its icy fingers grip my naked legs. Cold slivers worm their way into the tops of my boots and the lower half of my body gradually becomes senseless as we continue forward, our laboured steps the only sound. Even the blackbird has given up. The stranger is determined and unyielding. When I let my feet drag in a futile effort to rest, he shakes me hard and pours more whisky into my mouth.

'I want to sleep,' I splutter, pushing him away.

'If you sleep you'll die.'

'I wanted to die.'

He doesn't reply.

He is strong. I let my head fall against his shoulder but as I study the erratic movement of my limbs, my balance goes again and I stumble heavily into a deep drift. My face hits the snow and my eyes close.

A stinging slap around the face wakes me. He's above me, shaking, kicking, shouting. I reach out and blindly try to hit him back.

'Get up!'

'Let me sleep. I want to sleep.'

'I said get up!'

He takes my upper arms and hauls me to my feet. 'What in the hell happened to you?' His face is only inches from mine and the condensation from his breath folds into my own. 'Tell me.'

I shake my head and look at him through half-closed eyes. His expression is grim and frustrated. He pulls me against him once more and we stumble on.

Eventually we reach flatter, easier land. I make out a sweeping plain of dirty whites, criss-crossed here and there by wire and fence post. An angry, grey sky breathes down on the horizon and small white flecks spiral before my eyes. The cold has refuelled itself and a whispering blizzard has begun to engulf the oncoming night. My legs have lost whatever feeling they'd regained. As they buckle beneath me, his arms take the full weight of my body and he begins carrying me like a child, my head bumping against his shoulder.

As I pass in and out of consciousness, I'm aware of him murmuring, but his words are indistinguishable. I'm in his arms and through the final trudge of this terrible journey I can hear the breath tearing from his exhausted body. Then I'm not even aware of that.

When I wake there are voices, his voice and another, gruffer one, which I can barely understand.

'Where's my dad?'

''Ee's in th'ouse.'

'Get him, can you?'

Hurried footsteps crunch on snow. My head is pressed into his shoulder. I can no longer move, cannot raise my head to see who these people are. I hear another voice: soft and enquiring.

'Where did you find her?'

'By the river.'

'We've got to get her inside. Art, call an ambulance.'

'S'no good, John. Nothin's gonna get through till Barnes gets the ploughs out.'

'Let's get her inside anyway.'

I feel several pairs of hands on me and suddenly I'm being carried along like a coffin in a procession. I start to faint again, the life seeping imperceptibly from my body and this time, because I'm sure I will die, I say it quietly. So quietly I'm sure nobody will hear.

'Nicola,' I say. 'My name is Nicola.'

Chapter Two

The urgent cry of a cockerel occasionally filters through this stubborn wall of sleep. I'm aware from day to day, hour to hour, minute to minute – which timescale I'm not exactly sure – of small sounds, home sounds, farm sounds: the lowing of a cow; the sweeping of a brush on concrete; the roar of a tractor's engine. Sounds that tickle the edge of my consciousness, fall away, return, fall away. Sleep sucks at me, I'm a pushover for sleep. I welcome its warm embrace, its entwining arm.

I resist the temptation to open my eyes. I'm aware that I am alive, that my senses are intact, but when I open my eyes there will be questions, questions I do not want to answer.

Instead I let my fingers explore the cotton corners of a pillow, the fat ridge of a quilt. They stroke the smooth surface of crisp sheets then move to my own body, my skin under a foreign nightdress, my arms and legs still faintly plump. I squeeze and manipulate, in awe of the body I still possess. I stroke my hair, the long strands dry and broken under my finger tips. Only when I'm assured of my own being do I finally open my eyes.

I survey the room. It's white with a faded pink carpet and low beams which grip the eaves. It has a small latticed window, its frames bubbled with yellowing paint. Above me is a large crack in the ceiling. The wallpaper is discoloured, nicotine-brown curdled with white. There are pictures, each one is a version of the same bird, its feathers a rich reddish-brown plume – a bird of prey.

Turning my head to the wall, I think of another room, of a telephone ringing unanswered, fingers working through letters and diaries. How long until the unpaid bills arrive, the creditors from the agency? Then I wonder who exactly will miss me. I have few friends, he saw to that. Oh yes, I have no doubt of that.

Footsteps approach my door, they are light and clipped.

He doesn't knock but walks straight in. Does he presume I am still asleep? Seeing my eyes are open he gives a start and smiles.

'Well, hello. I see you're back in the land of the living.'

This is not the man who rescued me. The one who enters my room now is older, frailer. With a shock I realise I'm disappointed. I have looked forward to this intrusion without knowing it. Somehow, during my unconsciousness, there has been a sustained vision of determined eyes, a strong arm dragging me, confused words ....

This man pauses at the door. His tired face is lean, the cheekbones and forehead high, his mouth thin. He wears gold-rimmed, crescent-shaped glasses which are positioned half way down his small, straight nose.

'That was a very doctorish thing to say,' I whisper huskily.

'Well, I am one, you know.'

His eyes betray his tired appearance. While the rest of him gives the look of weariness and defeat, those cool blue irises are intent. They are small, and surrounded by fine, ragged lines. He moves forward with light steps and leans over me. Fine silver hair slides over his narrow brow and I notice the scars which cruelly mark his face. There are three: one on his forehead, travelling from his left temple to his right eye, two more cut across his cheek. They're deep. Healed, but deep.

He reaches out a hand and presses it against my forehead.

'You must be built of strong stuff. I thought you wouldn't pull through. Can you put this in your mouth?'

He places a thermometer under my tongue.

'We couldn't get you to the hospital, I'm afraid. There's chaos on the roads. We've had the worst blizzards for forty years.'

The voice is gentle, educated.

'So you are Nicola.'

'Umhmm.'

'You have been very sick. Where on earth did you appear from?'

I motion to the thermometer with my eyes. He smiles at me from under his glasses and looks at his watch.

'How's your appetite, could you eat something?'

I shake my head.

'Soup? Something liquid. You must eat, you know. You've not had a thing for days.'

He takes the thermometer from my mouth, reads it, and puts it on a table beside the bed.

'That looks better. You've had pneumonia. How long were you out there?'

I shrug. 'I don't know. A day, something like that ....'

'You wanted to kill yourself.'

'Yes.'

'Now why would a pretty young woman like you want to do that?'

I turn my head away from him, my eyes staring at the yellowing wall. Why does he do this, calling me *pretty*? Can't he see it's too late to tell me my worth, can't he see I have no worth?

He looks at me with a concerned expression.

'Is there anyone we can contact for you? Family? You had no identification on you, no mobile phone or anything. Not even a bag. I checked with the police. They are going to come and speak to you when you're a bit better.'

I struggle to raise my head.

'Please try to be still, you'll get your strength back soon enough. The antibiotics are beating the infection now.'

He rises.

'Is there anyone?'

I shake my head.

'Please,' I say quietly. 'Please don't get the police. There's no need. There's no need,' I repeat. 'And I really don't want them involved.'

He looks at me a moment longer and shrugs. 'Whatever you say. You're not a child.'

'Thank you.'

'Don't thank me,' he says softly. 'Thank my son. He's the one who saved your life.'

The next morning, he arrives with a bowl of something steaming. I'm awake and waiting for him, my body propped up by the pillows, the dizziness past. He moves over to the window first and draws back the curtain. A thin light coats the walls.

'Snow's beginning to thaw at last.'

He smiles at me and I notice he's wearing the same clothes as yesterday. Placing the soup carefully on the table he sits down on the bed, the V-necked, cotton jumper wrinkling around his thin waist. He says nothing, staring down at my face with concern. Then he feels my forehead.

'You look better.'

I nod. 'I feel it.'

'See if you can manage some of this.'

He lifts a spoonful of the soup and looks at me closely. He puts it in my mouth and I swallow the hot, beefy-tasting liquid.

As I eat, I notice how tired his face looks, the bruised and battered appearance of his skin. There are flecks of broken veins around his nose and mouth and the insides of his eyes are unhealthily pale. His bone structure, however, hints that he was probably once quite a distinguished-looking man. His features are aquiline, what people of his class would call well-bred, but partially hidden now by grey stubble and the unsightly scars.

In turn, he is appraising my face with the same level of attention, those cool eyes quietly absorbing my features.

Finally he puts down the soup and sighs.

'Well Nicola. It seems to me that you are on the mend. How do you feel?'

'All right, I guess.'

He places the thermometer in my mouth and rubs his chin thoughtfully. Growth crackles under his fingers.

'Your temperature is almost normal.'

'Where am I?'

'You're at Morton Farm.'

'Morton Farm?'

'The back of beyond.'

He smiles faintly.

'We're seven miles from Salisbury. You know Salisbury?'

I shake my head. 'I know of it. I've never been there. Who are you?'

'Morgan,' he says, still smiling. 'John Morgan.'

'You're a doctor?'

'That's correct. I told you yesterday, don't you remember?'

'Yes.'

'And who are you?'

I let my head fall to one side and yawn heavily.

'You don't want to tell me?'

'I'm Nicola.'

'Do you have a surname?'

'I had such terrible dreams.'

'You were delirious.'

'Wolves. Being chased … I couldn't stop running. So tired.'

I press my face into my hands.

'Please don't get the police,' I say quietly.

I can hear his breathing, slow and heavy as he sits beside me.

'Thank you,' I say. 'As soon as I'm better I'll find a way to repay you. I'll leave, there won't be a problem. I just don't want to involve you.'

I drop my hands and stare at him.

He stares back, and nods.

'But what about your family?'

'My family are dead. To me, anyway.'

'All of them? No aunts, uncles – nobody at all? Someone out there must care about you.'

'No one that matters.'

'Where are you from? How did you end up by the river – on our land? I know you're not from Morton, I've been asking around. How did you get here?'

'I walked.'

'But from where?'

'From the road.'

'The Salisbury road?'

'I suppose that was it – it was a busy road.'

'You had a car?'

'Dr Morgan. Please ....'

'You don't want to talk. What if I arranged for you to see someone? Someone who can help? It's a tragic thing, someone of your age trying to do what you did. I don't want to see you get better just to walk out of the door to do it again.'

'I won't.'

'How do you know?'

'Because I changed my mind.'

He rises, picking up the bowl. I watch him go stiffly to the door. He reaches it and turns to look at me thoughtfully. Then he shakes himself, as if a draft has come from somewhere.

'I'd like to be sure of that before I see you go,' he says. 'But it's better you rest now. There's plenty of time.'

There's something strange about this man, this doctor who is being so kind to me. There's a sadness in his soul, I see it. I see that, like me, he has suffered and appears to be very much alone.

Where is the other one? There are no sounds of a young person in the house; no music drifting from an unseen bedroom; no television blaring below. Why doesn't he visit me? After all, he half-killed himself trying to save me.

But only Morgan comes, regularly, morning and evening with various soups and stews. I feel myself gradually getting stronger until I can wobble around the room without help and get to the small toilet across the draughty, bare landing on my own.

Morgan doesn't attempt to glean further information from me. His manner stays the same despite the unforthcoming nature of this stranger who demands so much of his time. He remains gentle, courteous, but we talk little except to discuss small things like the state of the paintwork in my bedroom and the depressing weather, which doesn't let up.

'I've let things go rather,' he says to me one morning. 'This is a large house and I was never much good at DIY.'

He smiles at me constantly, and I at him, as people do when there's a strain between them.

I spend long hours at the window, wrapped in a woman's dressing gown, staring at a drab vegetable garden and a group of outhouses beyond. Apart from a rough driveway which winds itself away from the house to a gate in the distance, the farm seems mainly to consist of mud, metre upon metre of it, dispersed with the odd patch of green and the occasional, naked tree. Directly below me lies the vegetable garden. From here I can see the withered roots of untended, discarded plants which have obviously been left to rot, uncared for since the summer months.

I said that there was a reason for living, but that was on the brink of unconsciousness. Now I find I'm still angry. I still want to hurt – as *he* has hurt me. But what am I doing here in this house, accepting such kindness from a stranger?

Several days have passed since I regained consciousness. Questions! If I could just get out of this room and get on with the dirty business of living again. I thought that his questions would be the difficult ones – but it's me who's driving myself mad.

Gradually I find I can move around for longer periods without needing to rest. I look at Morgan with new hope, demonstrating my recovery by getting up quickly to open the door whenever he knocks. I say nothing, but he must see it in my face.

One morning he arrives with an armful of clothes. 'I found these for you. There's some woolly tights here, and a couple of jumpers. They're warmer than the clothes you had on.'

He stands looking at the bundle, then straightens and gives me one of his melancholic smiles. 'Of course, if you want your own things ....'

'No, they'll be fine.'

'How are you feeling?'

'Better.'

'Ready to move about, see the rest of the house?'

I looked at him unsurely. 'Would that be all right?'

He nods and smiles. 'I don't see why not.' He passes me the clothes and I lay them on the bed. I pick out a pair of jeans and a black jumper.

'Whose are they?'

'They were my wife's. I was going to throw them away.'

'Where is she?'

'She died.'

He offers no further information, but his face grows harder, as if a pane of glass has fallen between us.

He sighs and turns toward the window. 'I'm writing a book at the moment, don't worry if I disappear for long periods of time.'

'Really? What about?'

'Oh, just medical things, you know.'

'Don't you have patient visits, that kind of thing?'

'Used to. Actually, I'm more or less retired now. It's just that once a doctor, always a doctor. You see my meaning?'

I smile. 'I want to thank your son for helping. If I could do more than that, I would.'

'Yes. I expect he'd like to see you too.'

But he says it without conviction and remains facing the window. His expression is strained, but I cannot tell if it is due to the memory of his wife or the mention of his absent son.

'Is he here?'

'David doesn't come to the house.'

'Have you got any other children?'

'No. Only David.'

'How old is he?'

'Twenty-three.' His tone grows more guarded.

I look at the pictures on the wall. 'Where does he live?'

'Here, on the farm ....' His words trail off.

'You don't want to talk about it?'

'It's rather complicated.'

I push a strand of hair behind my ear. 'In that case, perhaps you can understand my predicament, Dr Morgan. I'm sorry I'm so ..., but it's the same for me.'

Morgan's face regains its concentration.

'It's just that I would rather not tell you anything than tell you lies,' I add quietly.

He frowns, pushing his hands deep into his pockets, and stares at me. 'I see,' he murmurs. As he turns to leave the room I feel that I have offended him. But when he turns to speak his voice is gentle, without animosity. 'I'll be in the kitchen. Please let me know if you need anything.'

I confess that I feel a certain guilt in leaving this bedroom with its peeling walls and its tiny window. But padding downstairs in these unfamiliar clothes, in this unfamiliar house, I allow myself involuntarily to take in a deep gulp of air untainted by sickness, that tastes, instead, of life.

I find Morgan sitting in a wooden rocking chair. He has a copy of *The Times* on his knee.

'You need plants,' I say.

It's the biggest kitchen I've ever seen, and also the barest. It's square, with a floor made of solid-looking dark red brick and a large, polished oak table. A wooden dresser stands opposite, its varnished wood laden with plates and chipped mugs. There is a letter-rest overflowing with bills at one end and a pile of junk mail at the other. A latticed window sits above a metal sink, with a view of the farm.

Morgan folds the paper and smiles. 'We used to have them. They passed away. My scientific skills don't stretch to botany I'm afraid. Help yourself to coffee.'

He watches me pad around the kitchen, occasionally pointing out where things are. Although he seems only half-interested, I know his awareness of me is more than casual.

I sit down and take a gulp of coffee. It brings on another coughing fit.

'You've still got a lot in your lungs. It'll take time to clear.'

I blow on the coffee. 'It's hot, that's all.'

There is the awkward silence of strangers between us. He places the paper gently on the table. 'Perhaps,' he says carefully, 'I should explain a little more about myself. I wasn't very forthcoming earlier, was I? I live here and David lives in ... well, I would call it a shack. It's at the other end of the farm, in the woods. He seems to prefer a recluse's life.'

'Why doesn't he live here?'

He sighs. 'I think you should ask David that question. Things have not been very good between us for some time, for reasons that are best known to David and which I would prefer not to discuss. In fact, when he brought you to the house – well, I believe it's the first time he's spoken to me for nearly a year.'

He pauses in order for me to digest this. 'I come from Cambridge. Studied and practised medicine in London and met David's mother there. After a brief spell abroad we came here, ten years ago, so I could go into general practice. David's mother came from Salisbury. She wanted to return to the countryside.

'Two years ago I went into early retirement – for health reasons mainly. I still do some locum work here and there, but that's about all. I have a man here who looks after the running of the farm. It's only a small place – you'll see when you're well enough to go outside. I sell some produce to the village and a lot of the land is leased. Life is fairly easy.'

'And David?'

'David,' he says, 'can explain himself.'

A silence descends. He takes off his glasses and rubs them absently on his jumper. 'I don't know who you are Nicola,' he says. 'And you don't seem to want to tell me anything. That's fine. But where will you go?'

A cockerel's crow rises from the farm.

I lift my head. 'I keep hearing that. You keep chickens?'

He nods. 'We supply eggs to the local shop.'

'What other animals?'

'Cows, pigs. We're not big. It's a hobby really.'

I draw a slow picture on the polished wood with my fingertips and do not look at him. He leans forward in his chair.

'You haven't answered my question.'

'Dr Morgan,' I say, 'I promise that I'll leave as soon as possible. In the next few days, if that's all right with you, when I'm a little stronger. As soon as I find a way, I'll send you a cheque to cover any expenses. I'm more than grateful for what you've done already.'

A knock on the door interrupts me. Morgan gets up rather tiredly and adjusts his glasses.

'That'll be Art – my farmhand.'

But it isn't. It's the other one. He comes in hesitantly, wearing the same green coat and mud-splashed jeans he had on that terrible day. At first he doesn't see me, probably because he doesn't expect to. He and his father stand facing each other.

'Came to see how she's doing.'

The younger man's voice is strained. He looks awkward leaning there in the doorway, one hand in his jeans pocket, his eyes averted from his father's face. Morgan stands opposite him, his narrow shoulders tense, his chin high.

'She can tell you herself.'

I step forward.

David reddens behind his locks of brown hair. I instantly recall him, the dark eyes, the hard mouth.

'Hi.'

'All right. You better?' He shifts slightly as he speaks and pushes a hand through his thick, curly hair.

'Yes.' My voice falls. 'I'm sorry you found me like that.'

'It's good job I did. You were lucky. I came down to photograph an animal, a bird, it's for my painting – in the snow and everything. You know.'

'The bird in the pictures?'

'In my old bedroom – the attic room?'

I nod.

'You saw them?' His face brightens. 'Did you like them? She's mine. The bird I mean. I trained her. You'll have to come and see her.'

'I'd like to.'

'I don't think Nicola's well enough yet,' his father breaks in. 'She should stay indoors for a bit longer.'

'Well that's up to her, isn't it?'

The sound of his father's voice seems to shake David. His expression changes and his tone flips to aggression. He looks at Morgan sharply and turns to leave. Halfway out he pauses.

'I'll see you before you go?'

'Yes,' I say. 'I'd like to see the bird.'

'Sure, come up anytime.'

Then he shuts the door and we listen in silence to the sound of his departing footsteps.

Chapter Three

The young woman in the photograph stares back at me. Her face is in shadow, her eyes caught by a single light. Her creamy skin is clear and unblemished, framed by long dark hair which flows over her shoulders. She is fine-boned, her mouth wide, her nose small and delicate.

Morgan has left me to carry on with his work. Pleased to be out of bed, I have spent a while exploring the lower rooms of the house and now find myself in a small sitting room with shabby sofas and a small coffee table. Dusty, book-jammed shelves line the walls, the most prominent of which is home to this photograph. Outside the weather is still filthy, the sky streaked with folds of dull greys and bright ivory.

A car door slams. It's followed by the sound of footsteps. Hearing a floorboard creak from upstairs, I glance one last time at the photograph of the woman who I guess must be David's mother. I make my way to the kitchen.

A woman enters in a flurry, like a great wind bursting through the door. She looks left then right before she sees me.

'Well!' she says and laughs. 'Sorry to seem so surprised but it's not often you find another human in this place. Sorry to let myself in and that but John never minds. I keep telling 'im to get 'imself a doorbell.'

I smile politely.

'I'm Nicola,' I say.

'I'm Audrey. I've come about the eggs.'

She's a small woman with mousey-grey unkempt hair which chases itself around her round, ruddy face. She must be in her mid-forties but by the heavy use of brown mascara and dark pencil around her lips, she obviously intends to look younger.

'The eggs?'

'That's right. I own the local shop in Morton. Dr Morgan sells me free range eggs. I can't get them anywhere else, you know, unless I go to Salisbury. You know Salisbury?'

I shake my head. It's the second time I've been asked this.

'It's a bit far to go just for a few dozen eggs. It's my son James, you see. Gives me stick about sellin' battery ones.'

She moves around the kitchen as if fearful that I have spirited away the family silver. I sit down at the table and watch her.

'I see.'

The woman stops and gives me another once-over.

'John at home, is he?'

'He's upstairs. I'll call him.'

'Writing, is he?'

'I think so.'

'Of course,' she goes on, stalling me. 'He makes enough money from those books, you know. No need to sell eggs or anything else for that matter – but maybe you know that?'

'No, I don't,' I say. 'I've only just met Dr Morgan.'

'I know,' she says. 'You're the girl he's been talking about. Turned up on his land last week.'

'That's right.'

Her blue eyes harden. 'And won't say why.'

'This is between Dr Morgan and myself, I believe, Mrs ....'

'Burrows. Audrey Burrows. Dr Morgan doesn't often have guests, you know,' she adds suddenly, quite sharply. 'He's one of those loner types – you can see where the son gets it from.'

'I'm not staying much longer. And I've already explained to Dr Morgan that I'm grateful for his help. And David's.'

'Yes, well.' She recovers quickly. 'Of course I didn't think you were – you know? Not your fault there's been blizzards. Good of him, mind, to let you stay on 'ere when he could 'ave sent you up to Salisbury. But apparently the son was behind that.'

'David?'

'Well, not that it's any of my business, of course, but Art said David was 'oping the doctor would let you stay 'ere till you was better. And Dr Morgan being what he is, well it's the first communication they've 'ad since the, well, you know.'

'Know *what*, Audrey?'

'Oh John, you startled me.'

She whirls around to face Morgan, her mouth open, her face reddening as she realises he has been waiting silently at the door and listening intently to every word.

'I suppose you've come about the eggs?'

She stands there looking slightly coy.

'Yes. And there's a couple of other things I need to talk to you about.'

Morgan sighs. 'I take it you've met Mrs Burrows, Nicola?'

He looks from me to her with a grim expression and I can feel his irritation at the interruption to his work.

'Well, we've met unofficially,' Audrey says.

'Nicola is staying with me for a little while, as you know.'

'Here we are, fifty-five pounds and seventy-five pence. That's for January.' She hands him the money and he places it on the dresser. He takes down a pad from the shelf above.

'What did you want to talk to me about?' Morgan says as he hands her a receipt.

'Well,' she says, sitting down at the table, 'it's about David. He was in again earlier.'

Morgan raises his eyes.

'Buying more whisky. I know the two of you've 'ad your quarrels John, but I think you should try to talk to the boy. 'Ee's buying a bottle a day. And that's not including the pub.'

Morgan's face clouds and he shifts slightly against the dresser.

36

'No getting through to some people, is there? I mean, I tried to talk to him several times. Always walks out, just like that. Leaves what he came for and goes off in a second. He did the same with James just after ....'

Morgan nods his head.

''Course, I wouldn't want you to ....' Audrey lowers her voice.

'No, of course not Audrey,' Morgan murmurs. and I see that talk of his son is embarrassing him. 'Please don't feel you have to keep trying. You do enough already.' He turns to me. 'Audrey cleans for me. You've probably noticed what a big place this is.'

'You know it's no bother, anything I can do to help,' Audrey says lightly. 'You're sure about that, John? I really don't ....'

He shakes his head. I feel the depth of his impatience with this clingy woman and I see that now she has said her piece about his wayward son, he's expecting her to leave. Instead she remains sitting and her eyes narrow.

'There's something else.'

Morgan turns back to the dresser and replaces the receipt pad back on the shelf. Audrey watches him keenly.

'It's about McLaughlin.'

His hand stops in mid-air and he turns to face her.

'What about him?'

''Ee's gone to Chapelton.'

Morgan's shoulders tense.

'I know,' he says. 'I found out last week – from Angela.'

'You know already? Well, at least it's not such a shock for you John. Really, I mean, call me what you will, but I say it's ....'

'Audrey!'

They stare at each other in silence for several seconds.

'Right. I'll be off then.' She rises from her seat, gives him a final, troubled glance and leaves as quickly as she arrived.

I turn to Morgan. He has his hands in his trouser pockets, the same old grey trousers he always wears. His eyes drift over the red-brick floor.

'I have some work to do,' he says, and his voice cuts off any invitation to enquiry. Then he moves to the stairs, his shoulders bowed as if a great weight which has always threatened to drag him down has finally found its hold.

Chapter Four

I put one step in front of the other, half-blind. There was the night mist, or was it the result of how much I'd drunk that night? Probably. Of course there were doubts. You didn't go there this evening, why should you come here? I put one step in front of the other, each step of the metal ascent to my father's flat, and reaching the corner where I expected to see you sitting, I saw you sitting and you were looking at me with the same stunned expression, sat in the dark on his metal steps.

You stood up and you had rain in your hair. Looking like you didn't want to be there. There were no cars on the road and everyone was asleep except us. The rain hit you like a series of fists and you bit into your lip and screwed up your eyes. You wrapped your arms around your chest.

That was the beginning, expecting you there, seeing you there like a self-appointed God, waiting for my return from the shifts and the scars, battlefields of loneliness, my fucking father, waiting with your blue eyes all for me, and you reached out your hands, squeezing my waist so tightly. I laughed at the rain in your hair and told you not to wake him, but you just smiled and you told me I was beautiful.

I put on that long brown shirt and when I came silently back with my father's cheap wine I saw a hopelessness in your face, as if his bloody hands had taken me from your grasp, and I thought then that you might sidle backwards into the rain and the city and leave me facing all those shapeless wet roads and all the stupid faces I had to look at every morning when I got on the bus and every evening when I got off and every day in my empty world and every night in my filthy nightmares and it would all have been said there, in my shape, standing on those metal steps and looking for you in the rain.

You kissed me then, your lips like hot oil running over my face, your hands tingly cold on my back, pulling me against you. And I folded, folded because I saw that here was a chance to escape it all. But it was more than that, much more than that, and I knew looking at you that no word could ever describe that feeling.

Not even Love

Morgan spreads butter on his toast. He does it ponderingly, absently. He has been even quieter than usual this morning and I have begun to sense that this man is constantly absorbed by matters he feels unable or unwilling to discuss.

'You can take a walk around the farm today – if you want,' he says, breaking the silence as he stirs his tea. 'Not far, mind, just enough to get some fresh air in you.'

'You think I'm well enough?'

'I don't see why not. But make sure you wrap up warm – you'll find plenty of coats and scarves in the utility room.'

I pick up the breakfast dishes and place them on the draining board.

'You will see David before you go, won't you?' He's frowning at me over the top of his paper.

'Of course.'

'Then what will you do? Where on earth will you go?'

'I don't know Dr Morgan. But it's not so difficult. I can get a job. Meet new people. It doesn't really matter where.'

He folds the paper and places it on his knee.

'Doing what?'

'I don't care. Bar work, anything. I don't want to think about a career at the moment. I have a few qualifications, I can worry about that later.'

'What qualifications?'

I drop my head. He sighs but does not pursue the question.

'I'll need my boots.'

He gazes at me.

'The ones I was wearing.'

'Oh yes, your boots.' He rises from the table and moves towards the utility room.

'What are you writing at the moment?' I ask, following him with my eyes.

'Something a bit different for once,' he says over his shoulder. 'I'm looking into alternative health at the moment. May always pushed me to get more involved with it. She grew a lot of herbs, trying out remedies.'

'May?'

'My wife.'

'Of course, they're in a bit of a poor state,' he says as he returns, my tattered, high-heeled leather boots dangling from his hand. They're stained with white salt marks from the road. 'And there was a lace missing. I'll see if we can find some string.'

I watch him fumble around in a drawer.

'Here you are,' he says, passing me some orange bailing twine. 'Not very fashionable, I know, but it'll have to do.'

He watches as I thread it into the holes and tie a bright orange bow, cutting off the ends with rusty garden scissors.

I haven't realised until I step out of the great front door with its wrought-iron hinges just how warm Morgan's house is. The savagely cold air bites my face as I pull up the zipper on Morgan's Barbour and look around me. As I walk, the wind lifts my hair and sends it lashing around my face.

In the garden, a hen pecks fruitlessly at damp gravel among dead leaves which are no longer autumn's bright gold and russet, but a dark gungy colour, wet and rotted.

The land around the house is flat and depressing as it drags itself away towards the river, which is now only a faint silver thread in the distance. But the south side of the farm has a bit more character. Here the land rises behind the house, suddenly and steeply, its chest and shoulders covered in muddy brown woodland. A large electricity cable crowns its brow and a narrow road, barely visible, cuts a swathe through the blanket of trees.

I make my way round to the side of the house where the land is cluttered with the barns and out-houses. Beyond them lie some small paddocks, enclosed with barbed wire and posting. Cows stamp around in one, chewing impatiently on insipid clumps of grass which sprout from the mud. I wander towards them, my head lowered against the biting wind.

Morgan has not forbidden me to go anywhere, but I do not want to encounter any loose bulls or moody rams. Coming to the entrance of the largest barn and peering in cautiously, I see a well-washed passageway. A smell of dung and sawdust, almost a nice smell, lingers. The building is dark, the only light cast by open doors at each end of the passageway and one small skylight in the centre of the high, beamed ceiling.

A movement from the passageway tells me that something or someone is inside. My footsteps echo as I walk towards the stall from where the sound seems to be coming.

It's only a cow. She's rolling on her side and snorting softly, looking ungainly with her cloven hooves pointing in the air and her back wiggling. On seeing, or smelling me, she stumbles awkwardly to her feet. Her large, oval ears prick forward and her brown eyes watch me curiously.

Gingerly, I reach out my hand and make a clucking sound. Her breath, warm and damp, coats my fingers.

'That's Pearl.'

The cow pitches away at the sound of the voice. I turn to see a man standing in the passageway. He watches me without expression, one hand holding a bucket. He's short but powerfully built with curly ginger hair pushed under a grubby-looking, grey, checked cap.

'I'm Art,' he says, his head tilting. 'I look after the place.'

His eyes are red-rimmed and he has the face of a cold fish, without colour or expression.

'I'm Nicola,' I reply.

'Aye, I know.'

We say nothing, a strange and sudden mutual distrust of each other stifling our words. His studies me with his cold blue eyes.

'She's a prize-winner,' he says finally.

The Hereford is calmer now. She steps toward me once more and I reach out, hesitantly, to stroke her black nose.

'Don't worry,' he says, mockingly. 'She won' 'urt you.'

'How old is she?'

He looks thoughtful. 'I'd say about …. Let me see, Dr Morgan picked her up the year …. So that would be …. Aye, she'll be four now.'

My interest in his cow appears to relax him. He's on home ground here. He looks down at my feet as he speaks and I see his eyes light on my twine-laced boot.

'What 'appened there?'

'I lost a lace. Don't ask me how, I don't remember.'

'Aye, don' remember much, do you? Lucky for you we brought you 'ere – should've seen yourself: such scanty clothes in that weather. You were blue when I saw you. No wonder they're sayin' you're crazy down in the village, sayin' you shoulda bin put in a nuthouse place if there's nowhere else to go. Old doctor's so keen for company, mind. Aye, does look a bit daft that.'

He puts down his bucket and gives my boot his full attention.

'See if I can find you one. Kids'll maybe 'ave one. That's alright for the farm I s'pose, but not much good f' discos. Not that there's many of those round 'ere.'

'I doubt I'll be going to any in the near future.'

'Maybe not. 'Ow long you plannin' to stay?'

'I'm leaving in a few days, so you can tell the village not to worry.'

He sucks in his bottom lip and puts his hands in his coat pockets. His shortness does not help his lack of presence, especially as he has a way of lowering his head when he speaks, which makes him even harder to understand.

'Reckon Dr Morgan's got some ideas for you.'

I look at him curiously. 'What do you mean?'

'Well.' He pauses. 'Can't really say, not my business see. But see if I'm right, I'll tell you if I'm right. Not before.'

'No, tell me now,' I insist. Then, in a softer voice, 'I don't know what you mean, that's all. What ideas?'

He shakes his head and I sense the pleasure he's taking in this frustrating exchange. 'Like I said, I'll tell you if I'm right.'

He nods and turns away, walking back down the passage with short, slow strides.

'Hey!' I call after him.

But he carries on walking and doesn't even acknowledge me. As I watch his departing back, my mind is a jangle of questions.

Cautiously I stride past the rest of the barns and the cows in their tiny paddock and on into the patchwork of fields beyond. I'm not really thinking about where I'm going, though I'm shivering from cold.

Silence, wide skies, freedom. Standing here in this open place it seems to me that all my life has been lived in a closet: small rooms with threatening walls; fear of the opening door, shouts, and whispers. Whispers of wrapped-up lives; of hunters and the hunted; jaded hopes and jaded dreams, orders and instructions. Why could I not see it all then as I see it now? Why did they not put me in this great field then, before it was too late? Why did they not say, 'Look Nicola, look at all these ways to go. There is no single path, there is no fated road'?

With a shudder, I force my mind away from such thoughts. I try, instead, to decipher the meaning of Art's words.

It seems I have made a name for myself. The villagers, he tells me, are saying I'm crazy, that I should be in a mental hospital. I suppose I should be worried, yet strangely I'm not. What bothers me is Art's apparent conviction that Morgan's hospitality is the result of more than just good will. And yet I cannot detect any hint of malice or seediness in the farmhand's voice, he says it so blithely. He's not warning me, nothing in his demeanour tells me that I should be scared or on my guard. Art's purpose is simply to show me that he knows more than I do.

Besides, if Morgan has a use for me, why doesn't he persuade me to stay?

No, there is no justification for Art's words except that they belong to a man whose ideas still revolve around an ancient system, that of Lord and Tenant – a man whose life is spent watching the comings and goings of those around him. No doubt my sensational arrival at this house has given him and the rest of the village plenty to chew on.

The day is getting on. The light begins to fade over the tops of the barns, now far behind me as I trudge forward. From somewhere comes the sound of a chainsaw, a distant purring on the air. I should be getting back, I tell myself. Morgan will be worried that I've spent so long out of doors.

Then, high in the dulling sky, I see the hawk.

At first I think it must be one of those radio-controlled gliders, for it moves so effortlessly through the air and appears to rely on nothing to sustain its flight. But as I see the great expanse of its outstretched wings silhouetted against the bluish dusk, banking and diving as if carrying an invisible thread, I know this must be David's bird, that a glider could never turn with such natural deftness, such precision.

It circles above me in a wide arc, hundreds of metres above my head, as if heralding my arrival, spinning and weaving in absolute silence. I watch it for a long time, my feet turning in a slow circle. I look around, hoping to see some sign of David, who is nowhere to be seen. Then I begin to make my way back to the house.

We go to bed late. Morgan wants to watch an opera and it's such a pleasure to have the television on that I linger, enjoying the warm room and the sudden comfort of the box. Morgan is captivated by the music, never taking his eyes off the screen, even humming along quietly here and there.

When it finishes, he sighs and yawns. He stands up and switches the TV off. 'Well I suppose it's time to hit the sack,' he says, smiling. 'To coin a phrase of David's.'

I rise, muttering goodnight as he shunts fresh coal into the Aga, and mount the stairs. I'm exhausted, the day's walk has left me shattered. As I climb the stairs I feel my chest muscles cramp and I linger on the first landing, my body leaning heavily against the rail. The walls swim. I hear Morgan's feet start ascending behind me and push forward, forcing my unwilling body up the next flight.

Dizziness rips balance. Falling across my bed and lying there for several minutes, I realise my mistake in going out for so long. It takes many minutes until my head finally clears and I'm able to stand up and put on May Morgan's nightdress. I move slowly and my throat feels oddly dry.

Then I notice the book. It is lying on my pillow, open, its spine facing upward. I sit down and look at it, letting my finger travel slowly over its dust-covered green jacket. The title reads: *A selection of Post Modernist Verse.* I turn it over and immediately see the part of the poem which has been heavily underlined in red biro.

And what you thought you came for
Is only a shell, a husk of meaning
From which the purpose breaks only when it is fulfilled
If at all. Either you had no purpose
Or the purpose is beyond the end you figured …

The poem is by T.S. Elliot. Underneath, in neat handwriting, someone has written:

'Nicola – he makes fools of us both, doesn't he?'

I read the note countless times. The soft glow of the table lamp does nothing to allay a chill which gradually climbs my spine and lingers at the back of my skull. One hand grips the edge of the bedside table, the other carefully, thoughtfully, fingers the handwritten letters.

'… he makes fools of us both, doesn't he?'

The table clock's soft ticking is the only sound. The farm is silent. I lift my eyes and stare briefly into the darkness beyond the window. It's a clear night, the moon poised high over a trail of silver-streaked charcoal cloud, turning, folding.

'And what you thought you came for is just a husk of meaning …'

He has been here. He watched me leave the house. Does Morgan know, or did he creep silently past the office door, every nerve alert and ready for a confrontation? Did he sit here, on the side of his old bed and write this with shaking hands? I saw the hawk. Where was he when I was watching her?

What on earth has possessed him to do this? What possible motive could he have for going to such effort? And to teach me what, to warn me about what? Surely I have enough on my mind without this?

But Art's words earlier today? David and Art, in the same evening, both relating some inarticulate, muddled warning, about Morgan.

I lie back on the bed and stare up at the yellowing paint. In my mind's eye I can see Morgan's face, the eyes sad and defeated, intimating nothing. In a few days I will leave this farm. Morgan has done nothing to prevent it, but neither has he done anything to encourage it. He has not interfered in any way. Are these the workings of a devious man?

After several minutes I reach out wearily and switch off the table lamp. Then I place the book on the bedside table. I stare at it through the room's darkness.

I can see David's dark features. In this room a sense of him lingers. Soft brown eyes consider me from a dark corner, a hand sweeps through rough hair. Why does Morgan's son hate him so much? When he came here he could barely look at his father, his eyes screwed up and his mouth twisting at the sound of Morgan's voice.

I grow tired as the thoughts, more and more disjointed, roll around in my head. The conundrum merges, falls into one: David's voice; Morgan's voice. Then it disperses again into hard fact, making my body jolt and my head rise with a jerk. Again tiredness overlaps and fuses, drawing me down into peaceful depths. Until its gentle wave takes me.

I do not dream of David or Morgan, I dream only of the river and its constant mutter of silt and broken stones.

The following evening it rains. Hard sheets of it hammer the house and windows in an unceasing downpour. Outside, the fields weave and shimmer. I watch them from the kitchen window.

I am wearing one of May Morgan's dressing gowns. My walk of yesterday has taken its toll and I awoke this morning to a grim-faced Morgan proffering a bottle of the rancid-tasting brown medicine.

'No more walks for you young lady, not for a few days, anyway.'

I absorb the catharsis of the rain, the explosion, the final bursting and the thundering sky relieving its burden: cracks of blue, small clouds of light, fast moving, free of their weight at last; the river banks bursting. I like the solid wall of water which pelts the house. I want to tilt my head back and feel it soak my skin and run down my neck and chest, filling my clothes and swelling my hair.

To wash it all out of myself; to be cleansed completely of my terrible deed. Is that what I'm looking for? I'm certainly not going the right way about it.

'Nicola. Why are you standing here in the dark?'

I turn to see Morgan standing at the foot of the stairwell. He has come down the stairs as the last finger of light drops from the horizon. His voice, gentle and surprised, jolts me out of my meditations. I look up at him as he reaches for the light, half blinding me. He examines my face with concern.

'Sorry,' I say. 'I was just thinking.'

He stays there for a second, saying nothing. He's been working all afternoon and his eyes are tired and bloodshot. Deep shadows lurk beneath them. He steps forward and smiles. 'We'll have something to eat. I'll see what I can knock up with my limited culinary skills.'

I shake my head and move away from the window, the dressing gown dragging behind me. 'I'll do it.'

'You should rest. Why don't you watch television or read a book, you must be terribly bored sitting around all day.'

'I want to do it. I need something to occupy me.'

I move about the kitchen, taking down utensils and digging in the larder for vegetables. Outside a wind has risen and fresh drops of rain splatter the latticed window panes. Morgan moves over to draw the curtains.

'Terrible night.'

I nod but do not reply. He watches in silence as I prepare the food, lightly frying the vegetables in soy sauce and garlic and grilling some fresh fish bought from Salisbury Market.

'You like to cook, don't you? So did May.'

May. The ghost in the rafters; the cold wind outside the house. Why does her name always leave a certain silence?

I move over to the drawers. Then I take out some cutlery, and place the food on the table.

'It's nice to know we've something in common,' I say. 'I saw the photograph in the sitting room – she was very beautiful.'

He eats slowly and deliberately.

'Yes, she was.' But he does not look at me as he speaks and, as usual, the subject is quickly changed. 'This is very nice Nicola. Please excuse me for taking my time, you've probably realised how pathetic my eating habits are.'

I watch him for a while then put my fork down by my plate. He sees the seriousness in my eyes and straightens, staring at me with vague surprise. 'What is it?'

My fingers play with the edge of the plate. I clear my throat.

'Dr Morgan, why does David drink so much?'

Morgan takes a mouthful of his dinner and chews it. Then he takes a handkerchief from his pocket and wipes his lips. 'Why does anybody drink?'

I shrug. 'A bottle of whisky a day, Audrey said.'

'It's a lot, yes.'

'Is it because of his mother's death?'

A shadow crosses his eyes and he takes our plates without looking at me. The drawbridge has raised again, the way it always does when something intensely personal is mentioned. He rises and walks to the sink and I hear the clatter of china being dropped into water.

Pulling May Morgan's dressing gown around me, I listen to the sound of the growing storm outside. A harsh cough explodes from my body and Morgan turns quickly, concern in his eyes.

'How are you feeling?'

'Still rough.'

'You walked too far yesterday.'

'I know.'

He watches me for a few seconds then turns back to the dishes.

'You haven't answered my question.'

He comes back to the table and sits down heavily. His eyes meet mine and a deep sigh bursts from within him.

'Yes, he drinks because of his mother's death. And he drinks because he's seen from an early age that it's a way of dealing with problems. Not a good way, I admit, but a way. David probably doesn't realise he has a problem because he's comparing it to one which was much worse.'

He has lost me now and my face shows it. He draws a cigarette from his pocket and looks at me tiredly. 'Check any pub near a hospital at the end of an evening shift and you'd be appalled by what you'd find. Some of the heaviest drinkers I know are doctors. Dealing with death every day doesn't encourage you to look after yourself, you know. In many cases it makes you more fatalistic.'

His eyes travel across my face. He lights the cigarette and inhales deeply. 'Death chooses at random. Often the least likely and least deserving candidates are its victims. If you see that every day – children dying of leukaemia, people in their prime struck down with some fatal disease – then you tend to think, 'What the hell, your number's up when your number's up.' It turns you the other way. It turned me for a while.'

'Turned you in what way?'

Again, for a while, he's silent, his finger tracing the dark scars on his face. Finally, he drops his hand and looks at me directly.

'I'm an alcoholic.'

He sits back in his chair, waiting for me to answer, but I remain silent.

'Of course I don't drink now, but I'm still an alcoholic. Like a smoker, one is all it will take to take me back there.' He pauses, his eyes studying the yellowing filter of his cigarette.

'It started a long time ago,' he says. 'When I was still at medical school. The usual thing: being an overworked student, cheap university bars. I knew then that I already drank much more than most of my colleagues – five or six pints every night was my average.' He shakes his head. 'After graduating I began to work in a hospital. I got better – my shifts didn't allow time for the pub, plus I was assisting in operations and even I knew better than to let the surgeon see me working with the shakes.'

He pauses, leaning back in his chair. A shadow of shame falls across his eyes. 'It really wasn't until we came here that the problem became serious. I had an easy life. May came from a well-off family. We had plenty of money and this place. I got bored. My practice finished at five and there was nothing to do except come home. The Swan pub was next door; it was just too tempting. Before I knew it I was getting smashed out of my mind every night.'

I stare at those terrible scars on his face.

'I have little self-respect, Nicola. Stopping the booze is the hardest thing I've ever done in my life. I haven't had a drink since my wife died, but every passing day is a temptation for me. The slightest hitch, the slightest upset, and I'm thinking about the Swan in Morton. Sometimes I'm half in the car before I manage to stop myself. Luckily I made such a fool of myself in that pub that I'd really be too embarrassed to go back there.'

'What about your patients, didn't they complain?'

He nods, the smile leaving his face. 'I told you – I retired early. You can't keep a practice going when people see you getting into a car so drunk that you've wet yourself and you don't even realise it.'

'And your family?' I think that as usual he will evade the answer.

But, with a grimace, he says, 'My family paid very dearly.'

'This is why David ….'

'Yes, probably. They say that alcoholism is hereditary, though I believe it's more through conditioning than genetics. David grew up in an alcoholic environment. The sad part is it's the thing he's always hated about me most, yet there he is, swaying down the same sad road.'

'And that's why he left?'

'It's related. But I don't want to talk about that. The reasons are too complex – and too painful. Perhaps David will tell you.'

'And your wife?'

'What about my wife?'

He looks at me sideways as if he doesn't quite trust the question or like it.

'How did she cope with it?'

'She didn't.' His words are weighted. 'She didn't, or couldn't. I'm not very proud of what I put May through, or David for that matter.'

I stand up and carry the plates over to the sink. For several minutes we do not speak and I become aware, once again, of the growing storm outside.

'What made you stop?' I ask finally, glancing at him as I scrape the plates into a carrier bag.

'I did it for May.'

'You miss her,' I say softly, gripping the bag in both hands and staring at him.

His face shows no sadness but I guess that whatever feelings he has about his wife's death he keeps locked deeply within himself.

'I am a doctor,' he says quietly. 'I can accept death. May's gone, that's all. I miss her. I wish her number hadn't come up, but it did. You don't stop living because others around you die. That's the strangest thing about it.'

He leans forward on his elbows and stares at the wall in front of him. 'You hear the person you love most in the world has gone,' he continues. 'But the gas bill is still there on the table; it has to be paid. Your socks are dirty. There's a dent in the car which needs to be fixed. You go to the funeral. Everyone's there.' His eyes meet mine. 'They're weeping and holding each other and telling you how sorry they all are. You read the condolences on the flowers and throw the earth on the coffin. Then you go home to find that the toilet won't flush and there's another war on the news.

'At first you want to be left alone with your grief. You don't want things to remind you that there's still a life out there and the person you love isn't in it. You don't want to write out a cheque for the gas bill when she isn't there to complain. You don't want to mend that dent in your car, you don't care about it. She would have done – she hated to leave things. But she's not here now, so what does it matter? You haven't got the energy. Anyway, you're supposed to be grieving, aren't you?

'It took me a long time to start to function again. But that's the way of things, you either give up or you go on. I have to make the best of it. The seasons are changing. There's a rail strike on the news, a new pop song on the radio. I have to accept that this is still the scheme of things and I have to ride with it.'

He shakes his head in that tired way which has become so familiar. 'What I'm trying to say is this. That the world doesn't stop for you. You want it to, but it doesn't. Things carry on. Things you have to do, chores, responsibilities. You don't want to do them but you must, even if it's on some kind of autopilot. This is the problem David has.'

He pauses and a flicker of life returns to his eyes. 'He's trying to stop the world. As if, by not accepting any future, he can bring May back, keep her alive. He's a child inside, unable to let go. I thought he would come out of it, but he hasn't, and I'm frightened that this is going to go on for the rest of his life.'

The speech has wearied him. He stops abruptly and rises to his feet. 'I've spoken for too long. Said too much.'

I shake my head and drop a cloth back into the sink. 'Not at all.' I shift slightly and run my fingers over the tap's smooth steel.

'Dr Morgan. How did your wife die?'

He bows his head.

'I'm sorry if I ....'

'No,' he says quietly. 'It's not. It's just that that part is still too painful. And there's someone else I must talk to first.'

'David?'

'Yes.'

My eyes widen. 'He doesn't know? Surely he ....'

'He doesn't know everything. Just his version of events.'

'And this is to do with what Audrey was saying?'

'Nicola. *Please.*'

There is a silence and I feel the blood rise in my cheeks. He raises his head and his eyes are filled with grief.

'I'm sorry, I just don't want to talk about it at the moment.'

I potter around the kitchen and wait for him to regain his composure, pouring water over the dirty plates and rinsing them. When I finish I turn back to him. He's still standing there, but facing me now, and his face looks a little brighter.

'So much about me. Still so little about you,' he says with feigned lightness. 'It's easy to forget that everyone has their problems.'

I make a dismissive gesture with my hands. 'I'm okay. I've just got stuff to resolve.'

'Was it a boyfriend who did this to you?'

I nod. 'But it's over now.'

'You're sure about that? What you did was pretty drastic.'

'He left me. It was just too much at the time.'

'Can I help? I'm a good listener, you know.'

'You're helping me just by being here, Dr Morgan.'

He smiles. 'I wish you would call me John. I'm not really a doctor anymore. I get tired of the title.'

'John' I say, a little awkwardly.

'Was this man violent towards you?'

I sigh and turn away from him. 'Sometimes.'

'Very?'

'I'm sorry, I just … I'm the same as you. I'd rather not think about it. Really.'

He watches me for a second, his face concerned. Then he turns and walks into the dark hall. Outside the rain lashes at the small window. Morgan stops at the sitting room door. 'Quite a night,' he says thoughtfully. 'The locals would call this a "blackthorn winter".'

I put the plates away as he scuttles coal into the fireplace. Outside, the rain pelts down into ever-widening puddles and the wind gathers strength. I pull one of the curtains aside, wiping away the thick condensation with my palm, and stare out through the swimming glass.

At the same time, as the wind tears across the bleak land, something is producing a disturbing whistle which rises into the air. It sounds like the high-pitched cry of a person in terror or in agony, a cry so shrill, so piercing, that it makes my whole body tremble. At the end of Morgan's drive a flock of rooks rise from the trees in a menacing formation.

I drop the curtain and turn briefly as Morgan rushes into the kitchen, his alarmed gaze meeting mine.

'What was that awful noise?'

I don't answer, my body freezes as the sound rises into the air along with the rooks – a blackthorn winter, the river screaming. Even when it fades, I do not move. I stand with my hands gripping the sideboard, my knuckles white and clenched, my eyes never leaving the unexplored darkness of Morgan's farm.

Chapter Seven

The ringing telephone broke through my sleep and I heard my father's voice. He knew who it was. I threw the duvet aside, tapping along the hall. Already my voice was shaking, the old me, the little me, who could not handle you. I could not find the right things to say and I wanted to get off the phone. Three weeks later, the whole thing was so stupid. You promised me!

And the hopelessness of it all. How could I know people who spoke with roses and fires and then left me drowning in the black waters of silence? Soft touches, dizzy hands, you said that you wanted the whole of me ... Excuses like ashes falling around my face. Oh I could see right through you, pluck you out of the air, dissolve the fires that made you.

But with your usual resolve, talking, talking – and I heard my father's loud stamping in my ear, smelled his dragon's breath .... That was my last chance to forget, throw you aside like a worn-out toy, eyes plucked out and limbs askew.

But no, with the child's eyes I saw only the single path. In my chest an orchestra tuned and I saw the door open, cracks of sunlight in the cloud, your voice pleading, fat and full with juice. I found myself remembering your hot oil lips, the Jesus voice in you. I loved you then, for remembering, even if you remembered to forget, and my heart began to lick its lips. It tucked into your words.

Chapter Eight

For a whole day the gale blasts, its furious fists punching posts out of fences and flinging trees across roads. On the following morning it begins to tire. There is still an odd gust here and there, but the wind is slowly losing its strength and the clouds their weight. By evening finer weather begins to break.

The next morning I wake to brilliant sunshine. Whether it's the sight of the window frames gleaming in the early brightness, or my white duvet, dappled by its rays – or whether I'm simply better at last, I do not know, but I have real energy, the rampant roaming energy of an impatient child. It courses through my limbs and sends me springing into my clothes and downstairs to find Morgan.

I bounce into the bright kitchen and turn to face him. 'Where is David's place? You said I could go out today.'

He looks at me over his paper. 'Not for too long.'

'I know.'

His pale eyes trail over my face with a circumspect expression and he plays absently with the neck of his brown sweater. 'You look better, anyway,' he says.

'I feel it.'

He rises to his feet. 'I suppose you'll be leaving us soon.'

'I've been under your feet long enough.'

'Not at all. You've been the least cumbersome of guests.'

He goes into the utility room and re-emerges with the red scarf. 'Here, wear this. And my coat.' He steps back, surveying me, his face anxious.

'It will be strange to finally meet David properly,' I say quietly.

The sound of the door opening interrupts us as Art enters. His cap is pulled down lower than usual and he wears a large black duffel coat. An icy, winter draught rushes in through the open door.

'Found this,' he says, pushing something towards me. He has an uncomfortable expression, as if he's embarrassed by his actions. In his hand he holds a long, brown shoelace.

'From one of the kids. Not leather, but it'll do – 'ope it's long enough.'

I take the lace and thank him.

After Art leaves, it takes me several minutes to unlace the stiff twine from the boot and introduce the new one. I pull on the boots and tie them quickly as Morgan opens the door. The winter sunshine fills the kitchen with strong, iridescent light.

'We've deserved this,' Morgan says, seeming suddenly, inexplicably excited, his face brightening like a child's. 'It's been one of the worst winters on record.' He puts out a hand and touches my shoulder.

'It's along the road, toward Morton. You see it? The one which goes up the hill. Turn right at the end of the drive. Go along for about half a mile. There's a stile. Go over it and follow the path. His place is up at the top. In the woods.'

'He'll be there?'

'Probably, unless he's gone to the village. If not, check the farm, he helps Art out from time to time – if he thinks I'm not around.'

I move to go past him but he touches my shoulder again, his brow narrowing.

'David may say things. Things about me.' His eyes search mine. 'Things that may change your mind about me. All I ask is that you're cautious in your judgement. You are only going to hear one side of the story. You should know me well enough by now to know I'm not an ogre.'

I nod.

'Just be open-minded – that's all I'm asking.'

I hurry past him, out onto the driveway. As I meet the pot-holed drive, I turn around to see him watching me. He wears the pained expression of someone releasing a nursed animal back into the wild. I feel a sudden, inexplicable pity.

Then I stride out over the vast puddles away from him, the gravel sucking at my boots. A lark sings on the bright air.

Despite the storm's legacy, this wooded part of the farm is still a beautiful place to walk. The lane is sided with young shoots of dew-covered cow parsley and blackberry bushes. I am surrounded by the tall, shining limbs of trees which spring from a carpet of brambles.

I continue along the road until I see the stile. It's barely visible, a wet, moss-covered step amid a high hawthorn bush and eager-to-pounce nettles.

I climb over it and slowly ascend, ducking under low branches and raking, thorny bushes until the path opens into a small clearing, in the middle of which stands a run-down wooden shed, its green felt roof slanting toward a low door. It's comprised of long slats of pale timber with two makeshift windows, one of which has a sill hanging at an angle below it, two rusted nails poking out of its side.

A string has been tied between two tall trees at the side of the shed and a pair of faded jeans hang on it, wet and still.

I move toward the shed, listening for the sound of movement inside, but hearing none. Pausing, I lift my hand but hold it there, suddenly unsure.

I knock on the door. The sound echoes through the forest's tall limbs. There's no answer, just the quietness, the watchful trees over my shoulder. Even the rooks are silent. I begin to feel uneasy. I knock again. A minute or so goes by. Then reluctantly, I turn away and start walking back towards the path, my face lowered, biting my lip as I fight my disappointment.

'You're wearing my mother's clothes.'

I whirl around to see David at the edge of the clearing. He's standing against a backdrop of forest, watching me, his hand clutching a sack. His hair falls down in front of his face in long, matted rats' tails and he wears a stern expression, his eyes surveying me warily.

Then he smiles, and it's as if an inner light illuminates his whole face, the pale skin drawing back over high cheekbones. It's a smile not only of welcome, but of hilarity, of merriment, like a shared joke already between us. His eyes twinkle beneath his brow. He pushes the thick, curly hair from his face then reaches down and fiddles in his pocket.

'Oh well,' he says dismissively, 'they were only rotting away in some cupboard.'

He strides past me, his boots tearing through the long grass, and I realise that this is a different man to the one I met in Morgan's kitchen. This man does not blush or lower his head. Instead he grins as he draws a long key from his pocket and pushes it into the lock, opening the door into darkness.

'Come in. Make yourself at home.'

I take an uncertain step inside as he bounds across the room and pulls a large blanket away from the window. It scatters a subdued light.

The first thing I'm aware of is chaos. He lives amidst a total mess – clothes, plates, mugs, and many other items litter the floor, underneath which I can just discern a tattered red carpet. An old mattress lies in the corner of the room with a sleeping bag thrown carelessly on top. There's a musty-looking pillow and a dirty blanket piled up against the wall. On the other side stands a table covered with tubes of paint and unwashed saucers, which are thick with coloured crust. An easel is propped under the window and behind it row after row of canvasses are stacked. The first one displays the head of the hawk.

A makeshift fireplace sits at the back of the room. He has made it using a long metal pipe splayed at the end, rather like an upside-down funnel. Below it, a frame of bricks surrounds a pile of dead ashes. Two dirty-looking armchairs stand in front of it.

'Sorry about the mess.' He drops the sack. 'Are you cold?'

I nod and fold my arms tightly around myself.

'Here, sit down. I'll make a fire.'

He opens the sack and pulls out several large logs.

'It must be a pain,' I remark. 'Having to chop those.'

He grins at me over his shoulder. 'I'm used to it.'

He finds a newspaper and begins wrapping it in little balls. I watch as he places the kindling and puts some heavier wood on top. He fumbles in his jeans again, producing a tarnished Zippo, and stands back as the flames begin to lick.

'Want some of this?'

He holds out a half bottle of Bells whisky, looking uncertain.

'It's good if you're cold.'

I take it gratefully and swig. The liquid hits my throat with delicious heat. He takes a packet of cigarettes from his pocket and offers them to me. I shake my head.

'It's my chest,' I say, apologetically.

He nods and lights one for himself. I move closer and sit down in one of the chairs.

'I'm surprised this lasted the storm,' I remark, surveying the shed's unstable-looking walls.

He rolls his eyes. 'I didn't expect it to. The trees give it a lot of protection though.'

'It must get cold.'

'Too right it does. She's up there,' he adds, pointing to a corner of the room. 'My hawk, I thought you wanted to see her.'

'Oh.'

I look to where he points. The hawk blinks at me from a makeshift perch. I take in dark, fearsome eyes which are tucked into the soft plumage of her brown speckled feathers. Sharp talons grip the beam, their tips ploughing into the soft wood.

'She shits everywhere,' he says as I appraise her.

I turn to him. His eyes smile at me as he takes a drag on his cigarette.

'What's her name?'

'Blossom.'

We face each other in silence.

'Strange name for a bird,' I say finally.

A deep laugh burst from within him. He lets his head fall back and roars.

'Blossom!' he exclaims. 'Blossom! Wouldn't it be a wonderful name for her? Did you really believe me? Oh wonderful ….'

My mouth twists into a reluctant grin.

'Go on. What's she really called?'

'Feather,' he says and explodes with laughter.

I lift up a hand and make as if to hit him.

'I'm sorry, I'm sorry,' he says, wiping his eyes. 'It's not funny I know, I'm just in a strange mood today. No, she's called Sara, after an old girlfriend of mine. Actually, even that sounds ridiculous now. So how's my father, the cunt?'

After he says it he looks down and his face clouds.

'I'm sorry. That's a bad word, I know. It just seems to come out whenever I think of him. No, forget it. Let's not talk about him. What about you, how are you now?'

'I'm fine,' I say, reaching over and talking another mouthful of whisky.

'You'll probably think I'm like him, seeing me drink this. Is it true what you said – that you were trying to kill yourself?'

I nod.

'Why?'

'No comment. Only, I don't feel like that now. So thank you.'

He's silent, puffing on his cigarette and starring at the fire thoughtfully. When he speaks he sounds far away, as if he's really talking to himself.

'It was funny, seeing you there. I was on a mad one that day. Drank too much I guess. And I just thought, Bollocks, I'm going for a walk; get a photo of Sara in the snow. Went miles. Just walked and walked.'

He slumps back in his chair. There's silence between us. He lights another cigarette and leans forward to poke the fire. I notice how torn his boots are, and the mud which splatters the faded jeans. I look around for a tap or a sink of some kind, but can see nothing.

'How do you wash and stuff?'

'There's a tap nearby. The old man used to keep some rare breed sheep up here so he had one put in. I've got a gas stove so I just heat up water in a bucket when I feel grubby enough. I like the life. I know it's pretty basic but it's good. Nobody bothers me.'

'Don't you get lonely?'

'I've got used to it. If I want to talk to someone there's always Art. What about you? I bet you get pissed off in that house. I'm surprised you've stayed so long.'

'I've not been well.'

'And Dad doesn't mind?'

I shrug. 'Doesn't seem to ....'

He looks at me soberly, his large eyes narrowing.

'Good of you to trundle up here before you were barely out of the fever, wasn't it?'

'I wanted to come.'

He sits back in his chair and looks up at the ceiling.

'Yeah, sure.'

'I did.'

'Fuck it. What's the point? Funny bugger, isn't he?'

'Who?'

'My father.'

'I don't know. He's been very good to me.'

'Yeah, he can be very thoughtful at times.'

But his words are not benevolent, instead they reveal a cutting edge of resentment. Again he has lost me. I look at him quizzically but he just laughs when he sees my expression.

'You mean you haven't guessed? Well ....' He stands up and moves over to the table, fingering the tubes of paint lightly.

'Just don't go trusting him, that's all.'

He sits down and leans forward, staring at me intrusively. I hold his gaze, then turn away, feeling colour rising in my face.

'Which brings us to the poem,' I say quietly.

'Yep.'

'Am I allowed to know what this is all about?'

He sighs, long and loud, slumping back in his chair and taking a drag on his cigarette.

'You're playing games now.'

'Am I?'

I feel his eyes watching me, a bright humour on them. He's enjoying this. Within only a few minutes of meeting him, I already sense the tremendous mood shifts that probably drive this young man. His tone changes from courteous to antagonistic in a matter of seconds and his eyes betray his keen awareness of the effect he's having.

'Do you know that poem? Do you read anything apart from gossip magazines?'

'Who are you?' I snap, 'Raymond Chandler?'

'Nope. Just looking for an indication.'

'Of what?'

'You.'

I glare at him. 'Then you've a pretty shallow way of doing it.'

That takes him aback. His eyebrows raise and his mouth twists in a way which is reminiscent of his father. I reach forward and stoke the fire.

'If you hate him so much why do you stay here?'

His eyes flash and I see can him building up for another round of verbal volleyball. But I continue looking at him and something in my face makes him fall silent, the rejoinder lost. He rubs his chin and sighs.

'To punish him,' he says softly.

He sits forward, elbows on knees, staring intently between them. 'It makes it harder for him if he knows I'm still around. Touches his conscience. I'm like the eternal shadow he can't escape. It wouldn't be half so satisfying if I just buggered off.'

'Punish him for what?'

'Ruining my life.' He turns his face away and runs long fingers through his ragged hair.

'How has he ruined your life?'

'C'mon now, Nicola. Don't mince around the questions. Just ask them straight.'

'But he loves you.'

'Yeah, right.'

'He does.'

'Even better then. If he loves me, my being here just out of reach will hurt him. And I want to hurt him. I want to hurt him very much.'

'But what can he have ....'

'End of subject. End of me.' He almost snaps the words. Then his face softens.

69

'So you've no plans?' he says.

I shake my head.

'What did you do before coming here?'

'This and that.'

'Oh great. So is this normal, you trying to top yourself?'

'Of course not.'

He turns back to the fire, his face chewing over my words. Then he sighs and lights another cigarette.

'You're well rid of him anyway, whoever he was. Got any friends, anyone you can go to?'

'Well done,' I retort. 'Like your father you appear to have guessed that the source of my malaise is a man.' I shake my head. 'No,' I add, suddenly serious. 'They all know him.'

'He's looking for you?'

The hawk steps sideways across the beam with a flurry of feathers. I look up to meet her gaze.

'You don't want to talk about it?'

'No.'

'Fair enough – It's all right Sara – she's not used to strangers. Shouldn't you at least ring your friends though? Let them know how you are, find out what the bastard's been up to?'

'No. Not now.'

'You want a clean break?'

'Ummhmm.'

'I can understand that.' He sighs. 'I know what it feels like to leave the whole bloody lot of them behind. Burn your bridges – that's what I say. I've got nobody to answer to any more.'

He sits back contentedly and brushes cigarette ash from the arm of the chair. 'My old man thinks I'm miserable up here, doesn't he? He thinks I'm wasting my life. Little does he know. Coming here was the best thing I ever did. I didn't know who the hell I was before I did this – I was just another loser. Now I know better. You don't need people. You don't need friends. There's no such thing. They'll all betray you in the end.'

I watch his face glowing in the fire. His eyes are shining.

'You do it,' he says forcefully. 'Go out there. Without them. You seem alright. Go for it, fuck the lot of them.' He passes me the whisky again. 'For luck,' he says. 'Mind you, I'm sure there's plenty of this where you're staying.'

'He says he doesn't drink anymore.'

'He says a lot of things.'

'He says he hasn't drunk for a year.' I pass the bottle back.

'Told you all that, did he? Quite the revealer, isn't he?'

'That's all he's told me. I don't know anything else. I don't even know why you hate him.'

'That doesn't surprise me. You'd need a whip to get that one out of the bastard. No, he wouldn't talk about that in a hurry.'

He pauses, noticing my curious expression.

'Your mother's death?'

'It's a bad story. I don't want to think about it at the moment – but you wouldn't want to know anyway. Really.'

'I know it's none of my business, but ….'

'Another time. Honestly, I'm not telling you for your own sake. You wouldn't like him very much if you knew what I know. I wouldn't like to spoil your grand rapport.'

I stare at him.

'He makes fools of us both, doesn't he?' I say.

'Doesn't he just though, eh? Doesn't he just?'

'I don't understand.'

'Oh, c'mon Nicola – Nicky. Whatever people call you. What *do* they call you?'

'Nicola.'

'Right. Well just look. What a smashing little welcome he's given you, eh? A pretty girl turns up at his house, all in need, towing his erstwhile loving son behind her. He's hardly going to throw you out, is he now? In fact I would say you could probably scratch a good few more weeks out of the bugger, just play on that ol' chest infection there. In fact, forget the infection, just keep reminding him of the chest.'

'I don't believe that.'

'Not him, you idiot. He couldn't get it up if the Republic of fucking China gave him a blowjob. It's me, don't you understand? It's me. He's using you as bait because I asked Art a couple of questions about you – I said I was hoping Dad would let you stay on here because Salisbury Infirmary have a habit of throwing people out before they've even got ill. Now he thinks I'm a bit smitten or something – I dunno, because I actually approached the treasured family home on your account, I suppose. And he's desperate. If we get to be pals then maybe I'll listen at last – via his cute PR girl.'

'But why hasn't he tried to talk to you? Why is he depending on another person?'

'He wouldn't dare.'

'Why?'

'Because he knows what will happen if he does.'

'What?'

'I'll kill him.'

This, naturally, is followed by a silence.

'Strong words,' I say finally.

'Maybe.'

'So you're not?'

'What?'

'Smitten.'

He throws back his head and laughs that same gusty laugh.

'Oh c'mon. I don't even know you. It's him, he's crazy, sozzled. The drink has pickled his brain.'

'According to Audrey he earns a fortune from his books. His brain is hardly pickled. In fact, I would say that your father seems like a very intelligent and perceptive man.'

He snorts at this and turns away. But I see colour rising in his cheeks and I know I've embarrassed him.

I stand up and shake myself. 'I ought to get back. He said not to go out for long.'

He sighs heavily and pushes a hand through his matted hair. The action reminds me of his father.

'I'll see you again?'

I shake my head. His face clouds. 'You're leaving?'

'Yes.'

'When?'

'Tomorrow. Or the day after. I don't to outstay my welcome.'

He turns and walks across the shed to stand in front of the dirty window. He has his back to me. 'Where will you go?'

I don't answer. He glances round with searching eyes. 'You haven't got anywhere to go, have you?'

'I'll find somewhere.'

'Sure.' The tone of his voice shows his disbelief. He comes back to the door and stares down at me. He has lost his air of arrogance.

'You just said ….'

'I know what I just said,' he snaps. 'But I didn't think you were going so soon. And I had this place, remember?'

'I told you. I'll find somewhere.'

'Dad knows?'

'Of course.'

'Does he want you to go?'

'He hasn't said. I really just came up here to thank you for saving me. I haven't even had the chance to do that.'

He waves my words away with a disgusted look.

'Don't be stupid. You'd have done the same. Anyone would.'

I stare down at the dirty carpet and feel his eyes searching my face. His body shifts awkwardly.

'Will you come here again, before you leave?'

I look up at him with surprise. His face is genuine, earnest.

'If you want.'

'No, if *you* want.'

I look at the ground and shrug.

'Okay, I'll come tomorrow. It'll be early though.'

'I'll be here.'

He opens the door for me.

'Some of his ideas aren't so bad,' he says.

'Whose ideas?'

'My father's.'

I look at him questioningly.

'Forget it,' he says. 'It doesn't matter now.'

'I wish I ....'

He waves me away. 'Don't worry about it. I'll see you tomorrow.'

'Sure.'

He steps back and gestures that I'm free to go. I stride past him and out over the bright clearing, turning round once to see him standing by the shed door, watching me quietly with an expression of deep concentration. Then he lifts a hand, slowly, in salute.

Chapter Nine

The next morning he opens the shed door with a grin.

'I've cleaned up,' he says. 'Just for you.'

And he has. The assortment of crockery, which yesterday was strewn all across the floor, is now neatly stacked and gleaming on a paint-free table. He has folded his clothes and put them next to the bed. Even the carpet has been swept clean of ash and fluff and a fire crackles in the grate.

He kneels beside it, blowing on it gently. He wears an old black jumper and jeans and looks like a pagan, or a mystical Indian with his liver-brown eyes, unkempt hair and guarded expression. There's something different about him today. His skin glows a palish pink and there's a smell of warm soap on the musty air.

'You've had a bath,' I remark, eyeing him up and down.

'Correction. I've had a bucket.'

'A bucket then.'

He pokes the fire with a metal tent peg. The room feels warmer now he has tidied it, the flames throw a bright, orange glow over everything. Even the hawk, high on her perch, looks drowsy and at home. Her large eyes are half-closed and her beak is tucked against the soft feathers of her chest.

David stands and looks at me warily. 'I've done something for you.'

He approaches a pile of canvasses. Reaching behind them he pulls out a smaller one. He studies it then looks at me. His face is uncertain. He pads over and puts the picture in my hands then takes out a cigarette and lights it, turning away as I study his work.

The likeness is incredible, especially as it is drawn from memory. It's in profile, the background dark, only my face is discernible as I stare into the depths of the fire. He has painted the strands of my hair with silver and white and my eyes in shadow, marking a striking contrast to my pale skin. The picture conveys a figure in deep concentration, almost pathos.

He turns and draws on his cigarette. 'Like it?'

I nod. 'It's beautiful.'

'Good, I'm glad.'

'Much more beautiful than in real life.'

'That,' he says, his eyes flickering over my face, 'brings us to a putrid quote about beholders.'

His expression becomes strained as his eyes meet mine. Then he turns and throws his cigarette into the fire with a violent jerk.

'It's yours anyway – if you want it.' He sits down in one of the red chairs and unscrews the lid of yesterday's whisky bottle.

'It's lovely,' I say. 'It's the nicest thing anyone has ever done for me. Really.'

I place the picture down on the table and walk over to the fire. He takes a swig of the whisky and stares into it moodily. He seems disappointed, as if he has expected something more from giving me the picture. It's as though in washing and tidying the room, he has compromised himself somehow, and now feels embarrassed at the obviousness of his own efforts.

We sit together in silence. He passes me the bottle and says, 'I'm sorry. It's just me, me and my work.'

'What do you mean?'

'I paint something and I like it. As soon as I show it to someone else it all goes to pieces. There's a shop in Salisbury that sells my stuff but I hate it, I mean, taking it to them. When someone looks at my work it's like they're looking at a part of me, criticising me.'

'I didn't criticise.'

'Good or bad opinion is still criticism.'

He stares glumly into the fire. I think how beautiful he is when his face is not full of mocking, when his brow is lowered as it is now, the long fringe casting shadows over his eyes.

'So why did you give it to me?'

He brushes some ash off his jeans. 'I thought you could take it with you, something to remember me by.'

I smile at him then turn my head and stare at the dull light which struggles through the filthy window.

'What's the secret?'

'I'm not going David – not for another week, anyway.'

He sits back in the chair. 'I see. So when was this decided?'

'Last night. He doesn't think I'm well enough to leave yet.'

David smiles grimly and lights yet another cigarette. 'How practical.' Sarcasm stings in his voice and his eyes narrow as he exhales a thick cloud of smoke. He stands up and walks quickly to the door of the shed, which he opens with a violent wrench. He looks silently over the clearing, his hands in his pockets. A moody sky hangs low over his head, its grey belly marked with moving wisps of darker, more threatening clouds. The naked limbs of trees sway lightly in a cautious breeze and the grass, dull, unilluminated, shivers silently.

'Let's go for a walk.' He looks at me over his shoulder. 'Not far,' he adds. 'I just want to stretch my legs.'

'Sure.'

'There's a path that goes into Morton. I normally go that way so I don't go bumping into the bastard on the road.'

I rise from the chair and move towards him, watching as he pulls on a pair of muddy black trainers.

'Right!' he says, standing up. 'Just the whisky and we're off.'

He picks up the bottle and sticks it in the inside pocket of his long coat. He closes the door and strides with determination through the long grass toward the dense wood which we enter without following any discernible path. Tall, sap-filled trunks of ash and birch embrace us, their silent branches absorbing our form. The density of the trees creates an eerie silence, punctuated only by the sucking of our shoes in the deep, black mud.

He walks ahead of me, his head bowed as he negotiates the path. I watch the back of his strong legs as clods of earth kick up onto his trousers and wonder what on earth can have put him into such a sudden, foul mood. He reaches inside his pocket for a swig of the whisky but doesn't offer me any. For about half a mile he says nothing, his concentration apparently absorbed in fighting the heavy ground.

We trudge on and I begin to sweat and wheeze. The track climbs higher and higher, winding its way between the tall trees, the darkness and the silence going on for an eternity. Finally we reach the brow of the hill.

David continues, apparently oblivious to the sound of my sharp, mucus-filled breathing, and starts to descend the patch which winds its way downward through the trees.

'So what's so had about me staying on?' I say finally, finding the going slightly easier now. 'Yesterday you were telling me ….'

'It's not you,' he snaps, turning slightly and looking at me over his shoulder. 'It's him, it's the way he's using you to get to me, it's what he's try – '

He stumbles and falls violently, his brief lapse in concentration causing his boots to lose their grip and send him crashing into the mud. He yells, his arms outstretched, and swears loudly. Then he lifts his face, now covered in mud, and glares up at me. 'For fuck's sake!'

I'm shocked into silence by the sight of his helpless mud-soaked body, his furious face. Stepping forward, I reach out to him. At the same time I begin to giggle.

'Here, give me your hand,' I say.

As I take his weight, he yanks my arm violently. My boots slip and I crash down on my backside in the mud beside him.

'You fucking shit!'

'You asked for it.'

We glare at each other. He's still lying on his stomach and I'm waist high in it. The rain has turned the forest's bed into a bath of wet clay which clings to our hands and legs like a sloppy cake mix.

Without warning, David flings back his head and his deep laughter fills the forest's silence. His hands grip his stomach as one shrieking guffaw follows another. My anger quickly dissolving, I begin to grin, and finally to laugh with him.

After a minute or two he regains some composure. He shakes himself, struggling into a sitting position and his face, staring into mine, is suddenly serious. I stop laughing, my eyes meeting his with wonder before he looks away.

'Come on,' he says sharply, rising out of the mud without difficulty. He reaches out a hand and pulls me to my feet.

'Bloody hell, you're filthy.' He starts brushing some of the mud off my Barbour with fast, impersonal swipes.

'You're not so clean yourself.'

'It doesn't matter for me,' he says gruffly. 'But it'll give the old man something to think about if you go home like that.'

The mud is wet and heavy. It clings stubbornly to my coat and jumper.

'We'll have to dry you off,' he says. 'We're near Morton now. May as well go there. I'll pick up some more whisky and see if we can get a lift back. What's the time?'

I show him my bare wrist. He raises his head, peering through the canopy of branches into the sky.

'Probably be around one. Art might be in the pub now. C'mon, let's hoof it.'

79

I stare at his figure, coated from head to foot in filth, as it stomps along the path before me. Never have I known anyone with such volatile behaviour, who can go from gloominess to hilarity then back again in a matter of seconds, without warning or any obvious reason.

Above us the clouds have grown heavier. The sky is marked with hurrying streaks of rain as we come down the other side of the hill. Then the woodland begins to peter out until it opens, without warning, onto a great valley.

I take a deep breath. Despite the weather it's staggeringly beautiful, a great patchwork of fields and winding country roads merging in a distant rainy haze. There is no meeting of land and sky. The weaving greens of trees and hedgerow separate the fields in an uneven pattern, here and there the redbrick of a farmhouse interrupting its random tapestry. And directly below us, the sleepy-looking village of Morton sits huddled in its wet womb, smoke rising from its chimney tops.

We resume our descent and walk into the village.

Morton is deserted. There's an atmosphere of expectancy, almost of foreboding about its quietness. The river which runs through its centre has swelled to take in the shallower banks and looks likely to spill right out and over onto the small village green.

'Comes down from the hills,' David mutters, noticing it too. 'There'll be trouble if it rains again.'

I see a sign reading: 'Burrows Stores and Post Office' in large red letters.

David enters the Swan impatiently and whirls around undoing his coat. 'Shit,' he curses, 'he's not here.'

The pub is virtually empty apart from a few people at the bar and an old couple who sit quietly beneath a yard of ale. A scruffily dressed man in the corner watches us shiftily as he sips on his Guinness. The landlady, a robust-looking woman with plump cheeks and blonde hair, looks us up and down.

'Been mud wrestling 'ave we David?' she quips.

He pushes matted hair behind his ears and ignores her comment. 'Alright Grace. Art around?'

She shakes her head. 'But 'ee's supposed to be coming – 'ee's meeting Paddy.'

David turns to the scruffy man with the Guinness. 'What time's he due, Pad?'

The main raises his head. 'Should be 'ere now,' he says grumpily.

David nods and turns his eyes towards me as he rifles through his pockets. I hear the clink of change. 'We'll have to wait then. I'll get us a drink.'

He carries the two brandies over to a table in the corner and sits next to me. 'How are you feeling?'

'You sound like your father.'

His mouth purses. 'Cheers. Thanks a lot.'

We drink in silence until the ruddy-faced barmaid, who has been watching us closely, comes over and picks up my empty glass. She looks David up and down a second time with raised eyebrows. ''Ow's your old man doing these days, David?'

'Same as ever,' David replies, staring at the table.

'I'll say something. I know it's a good thing 'ees on the wagon but we don' 'alf miss 'is trade at times.'

Her vague attempt at humour fails.

'I'll bet you do.' His voice is heavy with sarcasm. Her face reddening, she pauses before returning to the bar. She gives us a long glance and shakes her head.

'David! Bloody hell, I *thought* it was you.'

We turn again, this time to see a handsome, well-dressed blonde-haired man who has entered the pub. He has come to a standstill, his hand clutching the handle of the bar door as he stares at David with amazement.

'This is incredible, David. I'd totally given up hope.'

David shifts with discomfort as a young man strides towards our table. 'James,' he says slowly, almost warily. 'I'm surprised you're still talking to me.'

'Oh well,' the stranger says, pulling up a stool and squatting on it. 'I was a bit pissed off at first, but it's all been so bloody awful and time ... you know .... I saw you from the shop and thought, I've just got to nip over, even if the bugger ignores me.'

'This is Nicola. Nicola, this is James, Audrey's son.'

'Hi.'

James turns and grins at me, but at the same time he narrows his eyes. It is not a lascivious look although this man is obviously confidently aware of his appeal. As I meet them I feel my body stiffen. He holds my gaze, then turns back to David.

'So, what's happening with the happy hermit?'

David shrugs and says nothing. James gives him a stern look, then his gaze returns to me and his eyes search mine. 'So tell me more about this amazing girl who's managed to pull him from his pit. How'd you do it? We though we'd never see him again.'

'We just went for walk,' I murmur, meeting David's eye.

'I'll bet. Crazy bastard.' James throws back his head but there's a false edge to his laugh. 'It's dead strange without you around man,' he jibes, slapping David's arm. 'You're a cruel bugger, leaving me to fight the horrors of Morton on my own.'

'You're never here.'

'Too bloody right, no thanks to you. I was so mortified at the thought of returning I even stuck it out to do my Masters. You do look a bit odd Dave. I've heard that mud masks should only be applied to the face – still there's always ....'

'Alright James.' David half-smiles. 'Leave it out.'

''Course, he never used to be like this,' James says, rocking on his stool. 'Used to be a right little goody-goody. Football, all that stuff. Brilliant artist. Still paint, Dave?'

David nods and lowers his eyes. He mutters, 'I'm sorry James – about you-know-what. It's just that I ....'

James lets his fist fall lightly on David's mud-streaked coat. 'Come on, you think I don't understand?'

'It's been a really bad time, that's all.'

James suddenly lowers his tone. 'But you really should listen to your old man you know Dave. He's got a ....'

David rises violently to his feet but James, apparently expecting this, stands up just as quickly and clasps his arms. Several heads turn at the bar.

David stares coldly over James' shoulder.

'Okay. Okay,' James whispers. 'Enough said. I promise not to utter another word. For God's sake David, forget it.' His tone is gentle, and I detect something of the closeness they must have once shared.

'Look,' he adds, 'let me get you a drink. For old time's sake, if nothing else.' He turns and goes to the bar.

David sits down slowly, but he's breathing hard. 'He never learns,' he says fiercely. 'Why does he always have to do it?'

We sit in silence, watching as James hands Grace a ten pound note. He returns with three glasses of whisky which he places on the table before us.

'Look Dave, I said forget it. Don't get into one of your sulks.'

David shakes his head and says nothing. James sits down. He's silent for a second before his eyes return to me. His brow narrows. 'So are you from round here?'

I shake my head.

'Funny,' he continues, eyeing me. 'You know I swear I've seen your face before. Recognise me?'

I shake my head.

'Can't think – ever been to Exeter Uni – studied there?'

'No.'

'It's a bit rural, mind you, but compared to here it's a metropolis. You must come down with Dave some time.'

'Sure.'

'Bloody strange. Honestly, I swear I've seen you before.'

He turns back to David and the grin returns to his face. He raises his glass. 'Good to see you, Dave.'

'And you.' David lifts his whisky warily.

'We must keep in touch from now on. I'm off back in a few days but I'll pop back at Easter. Have a jar together.'

David nods and half-smiles.

'Art's here, David,' I say.

He looks up with relief at the small, red-headed man whose weather-beaten face has appeared at the door.

Art comes up to our table, his cold eyes flickering with surprise, first to James and David, then to me.

'Art,' David greets him, rising. 'Do us a favour, will you?'

'Lift 'ome?'

David nods.

''Ave to do it quickly. I'm late enough as it is.' He wears an amused expression. 'Been out playing' wi' the pigs 'ave we?'

David grimaces.

'Well, ain't difficult to notice, is it?'

We leave James outside the pub and Art drops us back at the stile. The forest trembles with an expectant silence as we walk to the shed and the sky is fearsomely dark, hanging over the tree tops like a great blanket. As we reach the clearing the first spots of rain pepper our faces.

'More fucking storms,' David says, rebuilding the fire as I unscrew the whisky and pour it into two plastic cups.

'Put this round you and sit down. I can do that.'

I pull the blanket around me and watch him hook a sheet up over the window. Our only light comes from the paraffin lamp and the restoked fire. Above our heads, the hawk moves along her beam. She spreads her wings then pulls them around her soft chest.

'She's getting restless,' he says. 'I should feed her.'

He goes over to the door and takes down a small hemp sack from which he pulls a large slab of meat.

'From Audrey,' he remarks, holding it up to her. 'C'mon then girl, grub up.'

This is obviously a well-established routine. The bird sweeps down from the perch in a whirl of feathers, landing deftly on his coat sleeve. She tugs ferociously at the flesh, flicking her head and watching me sideways, her eyes alert and blinking.

David studies her, absorbed, his face full of love.

'She was a mess when I found her. She'd been hit by a car. That wing was broken and one of her feet was mangled. If you look you can still see where half the bone is missing.'

I peer closely but can see nothing. 'It must have been hard to train her.'

'No, not really. Art used to train birds for shows and things. He helped me.'

I watch in silence as the hawk finishes her meal. He lifts his arm and she rises into the air, landing back on her beam as deftly as she left it. Walking over to a steel bucket, he washes his hands then brings the whiskies over.

'Was it good to see James?' I ask, though I can already predict his answer.

'About as good as being whipped by an octopus,' he replies with finality, sitting down beside me. 'Funny that he though he knew you.'

'Hmmm.'

'You really haven't seen him before? James gets around a lot.'

'You wouldn't really forget someone as loud as him.'

He smiles and does not pursue the subject. I sit contentedly, enjoying the fire's warmth as I sip from the cup and rest my head against the back of the chair.

'It's good to be out of that house.'

'I'll bet.'

He squats in front of the fire and looks up at me through his hair. 'So where did you live before you went loopy?'

'Just a flat. A one bedroom place.'

'Must have been a lot different to here.'

I sit back in the chair and play with the ends of my hair.

'Why so secret? Was it Salisbury? Bristol? You must have come from one of them to end up here.'

I don't answer. Outside the wind tears through the thick branches and across the roof's makeshift felt. Heavy drops of rain begin to splatter against the small windows. I find myself thinking, suddenly, of that other dreadful storm, that terrible, unnatural whistling sound.

'You okay?'

I nod.

'So what happened to it?'

'To what?'

'The flat?'

'I couldn't keep up the rent.'

'Ah. The reasons begin to emerge.' He takes another sip of the whisky. 'Then what, after you left it?'

'I came here.'

'But why? Of all the places … Haven't you got any family – someone who can take care of you? It sounds like you've had a kind of breakdown.'

I shake my head. 'Your father asked me the same thing. That's why I was so reliant on this bloke. There was no one else.'

'He left you?'

I lower my head. Several minutes pass. The fire crackles in the grate and the hawk, disturbed by the high wind, moves hurriedly along its perch. David watches her.

'I know how it feels – to end up with nothing. She's all I've got now.'

'Your father said you took your mother's death very hard.'

He sighs and cracks the knuckles of both hands.

'It was his fault.'

'Her death?'

He nods.

'He killed her.'

He pushes the thumb slowly along the bones of each finger, rubbing them, circulating the joints. Then he moves on to the wrist, pushing and manipulating, moving the thumb in large circles.

'That's all you need to know.' He stares into his empty glass, then rises without looking at me and refills it as I stare with astonishment at the back of his head. Sitting down wearily in the large red chair, he releases a long, drawn-out sigh.

There's a knock on the door. It makes us both jump.

'Who the hell is that?'

'Art?'

'He's at the pub. He'll be there till three at least.'

He rises and moves to the door. Someone is calling my name.

'It's your dad,' I whisper.

'What the …?'

A blast of wind hits the room. The fire spits, throwing a cloud of black smoke into the air, and the hawk lets out a surprised squawk. Morgan opens the door and enters, looking

87

drenched. He wears a long woollen coat and a hat. Water pours off the hat's brim and down his face, running under his glasses and the neck of his coat.

David glares at his father then returns to his chair and sits with his back to us. Morgan surveys the room, his eyes travelling from the hawk to his son, the bottle of whisky, half-drunk on the table. Then he turns to me with an apologetic look.

'You should come home Nicola,' he says gently. 'You mustn't walk back in this.' His eyes move over the dried mud which coats my jeans and boots.

I look with confusion from Morgan to David, who stares into the fire as if nothing is happening. I get up and reach for my coat.

'She's not a child,' the younger man snaps suddenly, without turning round. 'I'll walk her back when it stops.'

'It's not going to stop.'

'She can stay here then.'

Morgan glares with exasperation at the back of his son's head. 'Be reasonable David, I've got the car and I'm risking it just coming this far. She can't stay here. It's damp and freezing.'

'I'll keep the fire going.'

'And stay up all night? That won't do her any good either.'

David rears up suddenly and faces his father. His hair is pushed back revealing a look of bitter resentment. I step back awkwardly, sensing the confrontation to follow.

'What in the hell are you doing here anyway?'

Morgan sighs. 'Don't you want her to get better?'

David swings round, clutching at the back of a chair as if to stop himself turning on his father. He stares at the wall, breathing hard. 'Why don't you just fuck off Dad? Don't give me this shit. Who are you trying to fool? This is just an excuse for you isn't it? That's all she is to you. *Her... her...* Why don't you use *her* name. It's Nicola, and she's got a brain in her head.'

He clenches his fist and glares at Morgan. 'Why didn't you do it before, instead of helping some stranger you barely know? You've already destroyed all the people who mattered.'

The venom in his voice makes me cringe.

'David,' I whisper, 'he's only trying to ....'

'Shut up!' He spits the words in my direction.

Morgan looks away. The sight of David's hatred seems too terrible for him to bear.

'I didn't come here to argue David – or to snoop for that matter. I only came to ....'

'Like hell you didn't. This is a great opportunity for you, isn't it? Get a pretty girl in the house. What do you think she is, some kind of siren? I know you, Dad, I know how clever you are.'

Morgan does not react.

'Go on. Get out.'

He turns to me with anger blazing in his eyes. 'And you.'

He shoves me towards his father. It isn't hard, but it's enough for me to grasp his coat sleeve to stop myself from falling. He takes my wrist and flings it from him. 'I mean it. Get out. Go on, go on. Go and give him a full report. I'm sure you've got it all down in mental shorthand, what a cosy chat you'll both have tonight.'

He pushes me again.

'*Stop it David.*'

The voice is Morgan's. It has a hard note in it, a ring of authority I've never heard before.

David glares at his father, then turns away, his face flushed. He's breathing hard as he reaches out and takes a swig from the bottle.

Morgan takes my arm gently. 'Are you alright?'

I gaze at David with bewilderment and don't reply.

'Come on Nicola, we should go.'

But I stand firm and don't move. I'm waiting for David to meet my eye but he won't.

'David,' I say quietly.

Morgan shakes his head at me.

'David?'

He turns stiffly. He has tears pouring down his face and he holds the neck of the bottle tightly in his hand.

'It's no good Nicola,' he mutters thickly. 'Nothing's any good, not any more. Don't you understand?'

Then he lifts the bottle and flings it through the air. It spins, smashes hard against the table's edge, shattering over my portrait, which is still lying where I left it this morning. Whisky and shards litter my face.

Chapter Ten

I wake to the sound of Morgan's footsteps, rushing up the stairs. He flings open my bedroom door.

'David's gone.'

I raise my head over the duvet, blinking heavily. At first I can't take it in. The night is becoming no place of rest for me. My footsteps sucking into the heavy snow, the great, grey hounds, unseen, but I feel their constant presence, their hot breath wet on my heels, the rough of their shadowy hides circling.

'What?'

'He's gone. Nicola, wake up.'

I stare at him over the duvet, body braced and shivering as I struggle to pluck reality from dream. 'How do you know?'

'Art saw him, late last night. He said he was never coming back, said he'd had enough. We've been up to the shed and all his clothes have gone. He left the hawk in the barn. Grace, the barmaid at the Swan, said she'd seen him last night, late. He was hitch-hiking.'

He stands with his hand on the doorframe, breathing hard, his cheeks crimson from the stairs. But then, as his eyes flicker over mine, I see his attention is distracted.

'What is it Nicola? You look dreadful.'

'Just a bad dream. I'm okay.'

He lifts both hands to his brow. 'Why did I go up there?' he moans, his voice filled with regret. 'I should have known.'

I sit up and rub my eyes. 'You didn't go up there to annoy him. You were just looking out for me.'

'That's not what he thinks,' Morgan snaps. 'You don't understand.'

He takes a deep breath and sits heavily on the side of the bed. It's late, but the room is still in semi-darkness though the curtains are open. The dull clouds of yesterday afternoon roam the sky once more and tiny rivulets of rain weave their way across the grimy window pane.

I am slowly waking up, the dark shadow of the dream receding. The gravity of his words has finally begun to sink in as I recall the events of last night.

'What about the hawk?'

He shrugs.

'But he wouldn't leave her, would he?'

'He's left everything else.'

'I don't think he would leave the hawk. She's all he's got. Who else can look after her?'

He raises his head. 'You think he'll come back?'

I raise my hands.

'He's never done this before. Running away.'

'He's a grown man, you can hardly call it that.'

'He's a child in his head. He knows nothing about responsibility. He'll end up on the streets taking drugs or something. He's got exactly the mentality, destructive, rebelling against life and authority.'

I press a ragged piece of nail between my teeth, then look at it thoughtfully. I think of David's face in the pub, the retreating shadow of his eyes, his palpable discomfort with human company.

'He had a hard day yesterday you know,' I say to Morgan. 'It wasn't just the showdown with you. Like that Grace character at the pub. She was making references …' I pause, unsure of my words, '… to your drinking. After that, James came in and told him he should listen to you – that made him really uptight. Then you appeared. I think he just blew up because he couldn't take it. All of a sudden, what started out as a short walk in the woods turned into *This is Your Life*.'

'I shouldn't have gone up there.'

'But you did.'

'What about all those things he said, all those things about you?'

'Does it matter?'

'He thinks I'm playing a game.'

'Are you?'

The question shocks him. 'You really think that's what I'm doing?

'Using me as a go between? No, of course not.'

'I admit I thought that if you stayed a little longer he might start to open up to you. He desperately needs someone he can talk to. But it's only because I want him to be happy, not because I want you to act as some kind of intermediary.'

'He sees it as something else.'

'Do you?'

'No,' I answer. 'No I don't. I agree with you. I think he's paranoid.'

There is the sound of the front door opening. Art's voice echoes up the stairwell.

'What will you do now?' I ask.

'We're driving out to Salisbury, perhaps we can catch him.'

'You think he'll talk to you?'

'Maybe he'll talk to Art.'

He rises to his feet and looks at me, his tired eyes searching my face. My gaze meets his in a helpless silence.

It's early evening before I see Morgan again. He sits in the kitchen, looking exhausted as I make him some supper. Night has fallen and dark shadows spill over his beaten face. He has searched all day for David, he tells me, driving as far as Bristol, turning off every slip road to hunt in vain for his son.

This second week passes with bleak weariness. My certainty that David will reappear becomes shaky as four, then five, days pass without any sign of him. The promised period of reprieve is drawing to an end and it seems likely that I will leave the farm without ever seeing him again, without ever knowing.

The weather begins to improve. Spring is gradually winning over the damp stalemate, and with it come the fragile frosts which cover the earth on early mornings. Bored of being alone, I wander into the yards, taking care of my step on the brittle, slippery concrete. I watch the animals as Art tends them, his eyes flitting with discomfort towards my figure, wrapped in scarf and Barbour, leaning over a nearby gate.

The hawk is in one of the stalls, the top door crudely covered with wire mesh. Her discomfort at being confined is obvious. She moves about distractedly, rising into the air and hitting the brick walls before landing with an agitated puff of feathers.

The hawk reminds me of another time, an image of another cage with greying walls, faded curtains, eternal silence. Wandering like a blind woman around our flat, barefoot and desolate, waiting. Waiting for a key in the door, a voice on the phone. Such images, bitter memories, return to haunt me as the days go by and my hopes fade. I find it increasingly hard to remember David's face as the flimsy promise of the present is eaten away by the dirty stain of an undeniable past.

I go to the clearing, but there's no sign of life. David's jeans still swing on the makeshift washing line and the frost-coated grass, brittle crisp under my boots, show no marks of any recent comings or goings.

I let myself into the shed and look around. The remains of the whisky bottle are still shattered over the table and carpet. I notice the ashtray he was using that evening, sitting by the fire, overflowing with butts. His clothes have gone, so has the sleeping bag, and his canvasses are missing but there are some drawings left on the table, most of them sketches of the bird. There are one or two rough outlines of my own features. In one he has depicted me laughing. It's an incredible capturing of that second when I reached out pretending to hit him. So this is how he sees me, my eyes shining brightly from the page, lit up with laughter, my long hair falling loose around my head. Just another girl, enjoying herself. There's nothing of the terrible nightmares which haunt me, the menacing voice of the river.

There was a period – those first few years perhaps, when perhaps I did look like this. But I do not like to remember the good times – for it is they that make us cling to the bad. An 'albatross' he called me, 'the river woman'. But there were times before that, before the waiting and the unpredictability, the Saturdays and Sundays in bed with the papers, our insatiability, drinking each other's skins. And always his words, his touch. Like a class A drug, he was always lifting the fix. Was it so surprising that I found it hard to come down?

I put down the picture and force my thoughts back to David. Going further along the shelf, I come to another pile of papers and find a pile of poems, written in his erratic handwriting. Most are unfinished, experimental, with lines slashed through them, constant re-workings. But there's one, below the others, which is whole and finished.

I want a woman
who
Could arrive from beyond all those that I've known.
A woman with this, and could
with willingness and disgusted wisdom
sit in the cell where the mirror is blotched,
where distaining pipes hold damp walls.

Not needing to lie or persuade that it is mine by right,
I'd taste the fluid of her company,
while we dwell and share something
of the sickness of things.
We'd dig and bury precious items there,
seeds poked in severed heads,
eggs of dark birds.
Living intimacies coiled together,
all the dark voices that in secrecy are found,
those that remain
necessarily alone,
and those that should never, never have been
so thoughtlessly lifted into light, from the ground.

I read it several times. There's no date, nor a title, but somehow I suspect that David has left this for me to find. I put it back under the other papers and turn towards the rest of his belongings.

Eventually I come to a portable CD player which is partially hidden by scattered bedclothes and papers. There are several CDs lying around, most without boxes. Picking one up, I read the faded scrawl, 'The Best of Janis Joplin.'

I press the button and the melancholic tones of *Summertime* blast out through the crackly speaker. As I leave the shed and stand in the clearing, Joplin's voice drifts across the grass and into the trees beyond. It fills the air with its bright agony and throws out a warmth that the day cannot itself provide.

This place, I realise as I listen, affords David much more than simple solitude and peace of mind. It enables him in a challenge which I also share, even if he doesn't yet realise it.

That challenge is to live without a past.

Chapter Eleven

That was the best part, meeting you that day in the park; fat ducks on a sparkling lake. We had no money, you a student, me part-time in that most dismal of jobs, saving up to leave them all behind and you, you said I was brave, but lucky too with my pretty blond hair and edible face. We lay on the grass with yesterday's bread, your finger plucking at the plush blades as you watched the big one with the bottle-green neck.

'What a life,' you said, 'to swim all day like they do, chomping up bread thrown by mugs like us, who can barely feed ourselves.'

I laughed then, turning my face, slotting my brown pupils into yours. And you lifted your hand, stroked my cheek, smiling your big boy's smile.

Leaning over, (there was a plane in the sky), you kissed me, and I felt your heart pumping in your chest. There were children playing nearby and you said, 'Fancy one of those one day?' – and I said, 'Yes I do, why not, yes.' You were stern then, a shadow falling over your eyes, pushing your hand through my hair.

'You're serious about me, aren't you Nicola?'

And I said nothing, listening to the plane's drone, the shouts of the girl in the little pink dress. Because you'd caught me off guard, cornered in a corner, your usual style. But I was tricked by the halo of the sun in your hair, the gleam of your eyes and so I answered,

' Yes I am, oh yes ....'

I was nervous then, overdoing it like that. But you just smiled. You were lonely that day, weren't you? Jealousy was my strongest tool when you said 'Who was he?' and I said 'Just someone I met.' And that was the first time I saw it, your fingers pinching my cheek, a sourness on your breath as you said 'Some seriousness' and I said – again – 'Come on, you didn't call!'

Perhaps you could have ended then with your knife-edge words and your pinion wrists, but instead you softened and you said –

'Nicola, I think I've found a place ....'

Chapter Twelve

Someone is throwing stones at my window.

I sit up groggily, rub my eyes and glance at the clock: six am.

Another stone hits the glass. I get out of bed and make my way to the window. There's nothing, only the outhouses, desolate and eerie, touched by the first pink hues of dawn. Then I look down and see him. He's grinning up at me from the vegetable garden, his hair swept back from his face. The hawk is perched on his arm.

As our eyes meet, a stillness comes over both of us. His smile fades. A faint morning breeze rolls in from the fields and picks up his shirt collar, sending it in a bang across his cheek. He cuts a desolate figure, standing against a backdrop of weed and mud, his gaze lowered and still.

I dress quickly, keening my ears to the house in case Morgan is up, but only silence greets me. Even in his recent agitated state, I cannot imagine Morgan working at this time of the morning. I put on a pair of jeans and a jumper and make my way hurriedly to the kitchen. Grabbing a thick scarf and tying my boots, I turn the great key quietly and tiptoe into the peculiar dawn light.

He jumps out in front of me, a ghostly, windswept, mad-looking figure, as if time has placed him there haphazardly.

'Pleased to see me?'

He's grinning, his cheeks creasing into two strong lines. His chin sports a week's worth of growth and the darkness of his face makes his eyes look even wilder and more penetrating than ever. A strange energy hangs about him and his tall figure, laughing over me, is overbearing, disconnected.

I stare at him dumbfounded and wonder what has detonated this sudden explosion of good humour. He laughs loudly on the morning air. I lift a finger to my lips.

'C'mon,' he says, 'we're gonna fly Sara.'

He strides briskly away from the house, his feet crunching on the frost-covered drive. The sun's rays, stealing pale fingers into the purpling sky, have yet to warm the frosty morning. Our breath hangs in misty wraiths on the freezing air as I pull the coat around me tightly.

'I thought you weren't coming back,' I say when we are out of earshot. 'I thought you'd left me here to rot.'

He turns with a swing of dark hair and smiles broadly before walking on with a spring in his heels, his shoulders back and his chin high. We are approaching the outhouses. Animals' hooves tread heavily in the straw and a lowing comes echoing from the barn. There's the scrape of a pitchfork and the thud of shavings hitting metal.

David pauses and lights a cigarette, staring towards the sounds with interest. The hawk plucks at his hair impatiently.

'C'mon,' I whisper, pulling at his arm, 'I don't want to see Art.'

We walk on past the barns and stride out towards the horizon. The sun has risen and the sky is now a blinding, vapour-trailed silver-blue. I'm squinting against it as I watch David's figure spring along before me. The breeze bites my cheeks, and the tops of my ears have begun to go numb. I lift my hands and wrap the scarf tightly around my head.

'You'll be reading the Koran next,' David says, raising his arm into the air.

The hawk glides into the sky and we watch in silence as she wheels and dives, her long wings outstretched. David is filled with a dizzy happiness, a euphoria which burns in the crazy swing of his body as he turns wild circles, his head thrown back, following her flight.

I think of the poem I found in the shed.

'Go on then,' I say, 'tell me where you've been.'

'In Bristol,' he says, still spiralling. His dark hair flames about him, kicked up by the dry wind.

'Bristol?'

He turns to face me. His voice is thick with triumph.

'I've been looking for new outlets. I've found one too. Caplan's. They like my work. Really like it.'

His eyes flash. Then he spreads his arms against the sky and begins to whirl again.

'You don't understand. I mean Caplan's! I thought they'd send me out on my ear – especially looking like this – but they leapt on me, as soon as they saw the pictures. They've commissioned some landscapes. Do you know how much they'll sell my stuff for? Hundreds of pounds. Hundreds and hundreds of pounds. Wheee ....'

He spirals so fast that balance can no longer sustain him and his momentum sends him crashing to the ground. He lies on his back, laughing, the sky reflected in his eyes. Then he stretches his arms out by his sides to form the shape of a cross.

'Ooh, I feel dizzy.'

I prod him with my toe.

'So where've you been sleeping?'

'In a park.'

The question brings him back to reality. He turns onto his side and rises unsteadily.

'I missed you,' he says, his voice tone changing, 'I had to get back – before you left.'

There's something final about the way he says it, as if it's not necessarily a joy to him, but a fact he must accept. Then he pushes his hands into his pockets and lowers his head. His eyes search mine through a fury of billowing hair.

'And I want you.'

Taking a step away from him, I turn my eyes towards the outstretched wings of the hawk. My body stiffens involuntarily.

'You've only known me for a ....'

He flings up his hands in a gesture of frustration.

'So what Nicola?' he exclaims. 'So what?'

I shrug and look at the ground, wrapping my hands together tightly. He takes a step toward me and pauses. 'So what?' he says a third time. 'It happens, Nicola. And I can't stop thinking about you.'

I do not reply, do not look at him. I'm aware of his eyes boring into me. He lifts his head and watches Sara, her slow circles in the sky, her wings dipping like a homage, or an omen.

For a minute there's only the sound of the wind. It whistles in our ears and buffets our coats. I hear him sigh and his fingers touch my shoulder. A strange heat courses down my back.

'I knew it before, that's why I was so shitty. I'm really sorry about that. But I was scared. Not because of Dad, but because ....' He turns me around gently, so I am facing him. 'Because I always lose everything I care for.'

'Striking while the iron's hot?' I whisper, searching his face.

'You what?'

'Positivity breeds positivity. You're in a good mood today.'

'I don't understand.'

I shake my head.

He sighs. 'Say something Nicola, for fuck's sake. Put me out of my misery.' His voice is the old voice: insecure, desperate.

I raise my face to meet his and smile. I'm silent, but my eyes tell him what he needs to know.

'We'll go in a minute,' he says. 'Back to my place.'

'They'll wonder where I am.'

His fingers clasp my forearm. He stares hard into my eyes then lifts his other hand and runs it through my hair.

'Grace knows,' he says softly, 'I popped in for some whisky late last night. Anyway – I've taken Sara. Art'll have sussed it.'

I feel his breath on my cheek. He touches my chin with his fingers and his eyes seek mine. I search the horizon over his shoulder. His face is too intense, his pupils tearing at me as the morning breeze lifts our collars and tangles the hair across our faces. I turn sharply away from him and make my way across the fields towards the hillside. I can hear his hurried footsteps behind me resounding on frozen chalk.

We climb the rest of the path and enter the shed. David passes me a blanket then hurries about, clearing papers and stacking them on the table next to the oil paints. Picking up an old emulsion brush, he sweeps the shards of glass from the smashed whisky bottle.

'Fucking waste that was,' he mutters, throwing the shattered glass into a damp-looking cardboard box. He picks up the ruined portrait and turns to me. A shadow crosses his eyes.

'I'll do you a better one. It was only out of my head, anyway.'

He places the picture down and looks at it without speaking. My eyes are drawn to the thick mud which laces his hair.

'You filthy bastard, you haven't washed since you fell over.'

He looks up from the canvas and grins. 'I'll have a bucket in a minute, when I've done this.' He finishes tidying and then undoes a large, battered-looking rucksack. He pulls out an armful of crumpled clothes and the sleeping bag, which he throws on the bed, then feels in his coat for matches.

'Help yourself to whisky,' he says. 'It's on the table.'

He goes out of the shed and returns with a steel bucket full of water. Then he brings out a large, blue camping stove from under one of the red chairs and lights it, placing the metal bucket on top. I pour the whisky as he waits for the water to heat, drinking alone as he takes an armful of clothes and goes outside.

There's the sound of splashing water and singing before he returns clean-shaven, his hair in long, wet, curly strings. He has put on a floppy white jumper and a pair of jeans.

'You're smiling,' he says.

'You look like a different person.'

We drink our whiskies. We are careful now, sitting apart, our eyes meeting then glancing away. I feel no urge to approach him, our mutual distance is comforting. I sense that now he's spoken, made clear his feelings, he doesn't quite know where to take things next, as if he has not thought beyond that first revelation.

He sits in the chair and chats about his friends from the past and his school days in Salisbury. He describes Sara, his girlfriend from Morton, and I wonder if perhaps her memory is helping him find his footing in this new, more mature encounter. His relationship with her, he tells me, began when he was sixteen.

'She wasn't even beautiful,' he says thoughtfully.

'So what did you see in her?'

He pushes his hand under his hair and scratches. 'She was a childhood friend – and just ... normal I suppose. Solid but sensitive. And Mum liked her – that made a big difference.'

He leans forward and rests his head in his hands.

'It killed her when I finished it. She was really upset about Mum. She needed me for comfort as well as needing to comfort me. When I ditched her she probably felt so totally isolated. It was a shitty thing to do.'

For the first time, I have the impression that I am talking to a man of his age – a bright, well-adjusted twenty-three year old. The volatile, destructive streak which usually marks his voice and words is replaced by a sudden clarity and objectivity. It's as if the confidence he's gained from his acceptance by the shop in Bristol has enabled him to step back from his problems, to at last feel an empathy with others.

As he makes a fire, I take a walk around the clearing and enjoy the feeling of sunshine on my face. Small flowers pop their heads above the grass and I notice the first green buds clinging to the branches.

It's cold though, terribly cold, and sitting without a fire has left my body chilled. I go back to the shed.

'I was thinking though,' David continues, as if following a brief pause. 'It's good, really, that I didn't marry Sara. I don't know if I really loved her anyway. She was more like a sister than a girlfriend.'

He lights the fire, places on a few of the heavier logs, and steps back as the flames begin to lick. I move closer to feel their heat. He circles the chairs, sits down and reaches for his glass.

'But love is relative,' I say quietly. 'And cruel. People use it like they use everything else. There's nothing sacred about it. Probably you loved the girl, but it's not important now, to you anyway. That's sad.'

He looks at me uncertainly.

'It's the same with everything,' I continue. 'Pick it up, put it down when it no longer hits the spot. Not working so well any more? Not looking so good? Fine, trade it in and find a better product, like the most up-to-date ipod, or phone. Something your mates will envy your for. Why not?'

He raises his hands, which are stained from the mossy wood.

'I'm sorry, you've lost me there. What have phones got to do with love?'

I sigh. 'It's the importance we attach to things,' I explain, wrapping my hands together. 'Things of the here and now. Whether it's our present phone or our present partner, we always like to believe we have made a first-class choice for ourselves. And if the product isn't up to our expectations, well hey, both of them are to easy replace.'

He leans forward and kicks an old can lid away from the fire.

'That sounds a bit cold,' he says, 'and cynical.'

'It is,' I agree, looking him in the eye. 'But it's only what I've seen. If you hadn't spent the last year in this shed you'd probably have noticed the same thing. The whole cycle of sex and partner exchanges. People telling you they love you and fucking someone else the next day. It happens all the time. People are cheap – especially men.'

He raises his eyebrows. 'Phew,' he says with a wave of his hands. 'That shithead really hurt you, didn't he?'

I glare at him. 'Don't bring it down to me David. I'm quite capable of making an observation beyond my own experience, thank you.'

He smiles and leans forward.

'Tell me about him.'

'There's nothing to tell.'

'Oh, come on. Here I am confessing my feelings about Sara – yet I still know nothing about you.'

'And you won't.'

'Why not?' His look has changed to annoyance.

'Because my past is finished.'

There's a short silence. Then he says, 'That sounds like a crock of shit. You're in denial, that's what's wrong with you.'

'No I'm not. I know exactly what happened to me, I just don't want to talk about it. But if you don't want to live with that you don't have to. It's your choice.'

His face is disappointed.

'All I'm trying to tell you David,' I say, 'is that you probably did love Sara. Just because you don't have those feelings now doesn't mean you didn't have them then. You're not exempt from the shallow and fickle heart of human nature.'

'Because she was dispensable?' he says.

'Well clearly she was. *You* made her dispensable. You finished it because you couldn't deal with her feelings on top of your own. It's sad but true I'm afraid, the world is full of weak cowards and as far as I can see you have behaved no differently to them.'

I feel his eyes following me as I walk around the room.

'Bitter. Very bitter,' he mutters. 'Nicola reveals herself at last.'

'We have both been hurt David.'

He stands up and moves toward the table.

'You make it sound like some cold decision. It wasn't like that. I couldn't bear to see anyone. I couldn't feel anything any more. Don't you understand?'

'Yes, I do.' My voice is gentle. 'I know. Just don't make excuses for yourself, that's all. I'm talking about peoples' natures. How quickly they can forget.'

'I don't forget.'

'Of course you do.'

'Then you don't know me at all, do you?'

I sigh and sit back in the chair. He's fenced in, cornered.

'Face it David,' I say. 'You've forgotten Sara, or the way you felt at least. Sooner or later you'll have forgotten her completely. She'll just be some distant name.'

He turns and moves towards me. 'But I didn't ....' He struggles to stop himself from saying it. He raises his head and his eyes begin to blaze.

'You didn't what?'

He sits down with a dismissive wave of the hand.

'Don't you understand?' I say softly. 'The world won't alter for you. People won't do what you want because they're stubborn and pigheaded. Just like you David.'

'Why don't you just say it?' he snaps. 'Go on, just admit it.'

'Admit what?'

'That you're going to leave. That's what you're really saying, isn't it. I shouldn't get too involved because sooner or later you're going to fuck off.'

'That's not what I'm ….'

'Yes it is.' He stands up again and his face is black with fury. 'That's exactly what you're saying. That's why you won't tell me anything about yourself – because this is just a holiday for you. You're going back to him, aren't you?'

'I've no intention of going back to him – I couldn't even if I wanted to.'

'Don't lie. I've looked at you Nicola. Your hair, your face. Even your voice. Nobody leaves a girl like you.'

'I'm not going back to him!' I shout. 'Stop saying that. And don't be so shallow – people don't stay with people just because of the way they look.' I turn my head away. 'I don't know what's going to happen, David. Maybe I'll leave, maybe you'll leave. This kind of thing, it's always a gamble, always a risk. But maybe it's a genuine second chance – for both of us. Who knows?'

'I think you do,' he says quietly. 'I think you know.'

We stand facing each other in silence. He raises his hands slowly. 'So maybe it's better if we just ….'

'Just what?'

He sighs. 'Stop it now.' He lets his head fall and doesn't look at me again. He walks slowly to the fireplace and stares at it.

'Without ever knowing?' I ask.

'It sounds like there's nothing to know.'

'Oh, come on.'

'I couldn't bear it.' He lifts his head and looks at me briefly then drops it again. 'I couldn't bear it. I know I sound pathetic but you just don't understand.'

His face is blank and his shoulders sag. How quickly he has returned to his former haunted self. Only minutes ago he was sitting in this chair with a smile dazzling his face, hope illuminating his eyes.

'You don't understand the world. You're like a kid, David.'

'You'd better go.'

He turns away from me and lights a cigarette. I rise from the chair and glare at the back of his head. 'I mean it Nicola. Please, just go.'

'You mean you never want to see me again?' I take a step towards him. 'You mean never want me to come up to this shed and talk to you?'

'That's exactly what I mean.'

'No David, what you mean is this: that I'm just another person you've turned your back on because you can't stomach the thought of actually living again, of having real human relations. Instead you'd prefer to stay in this filthy place and rot away for the rest of your life.'

'If that's the way you see it.' He moves toward the window and stares out of its grimy panes. His hair falls down across his face and I cannot read his expression.

'David,' I say softly, 'do you think you're the only person who's been through the quagmire? Do you think you're the only person who's lost someone?'

He doesn't answer. I look at his back, exasperated, then raise my voice to a pitch which makes him jerk round to face me.

'You think you're so good, don't you? You think you're free of all vice, all blame. Dumped your girlfriend, dumped your best friend and shat all over your father. Well if that's the way you want to carry on then you can rot David. Just rot.'

I turn and yank at the door. It jams, then flies open. The morning's sunshine hits my face and at the same time tears well up in my eyes. I don't look back as I walk through the long grass towards the track at the end of the clearing.

I lose my balance and fall into the grass. The wet blades press against my face. I smell damp soil before he pulls me over roughly so his face is above mine. He looks at my tear-filled eyes with a kind of wonder.

Our mouths jam together, his teeth cutting into my lip. Then he's pulling at my jumper, dragging me over the grass.

Chapter Thirteen

He lights a cigarette, turns, and pulls the sleeping bag over my shoulders. My head falls languidly against him, my long hair spread out across the pillow. Above us on the narrow perch, the hawk sleeps, her eyes pressed shut, her beak folded into her chest. The re-stoked fire crackles and spits. We have lain in bed all afternoon, making love and talking as the sun's rays recede through the swirling, iridescent smoke from David's cigarettes.

I look at the evening sky through the smudged glass and feel contentedly aware of his warm body beside mine, the broad, naked shoulders and strong chest. I feel his breath sweep across my cheek as he strokes my hair.

'I knew as soon as I saw you,' he whispers. 'Even if your face was blue and you looked like a corpse.'

He rises onto an elbow and looks down at me. His face beneath the scattered curls is intense, slightly scared. 'Do you realise that I hadn't stepped in that house for nearly a year before that day I came to see you?'

A silence.

'What made you change your mind?' I ask finally.

'Change my mind about what?'

'You told me to get out.'

He rolls over onto his back and stares at the ceiling. 'It's what you said I suppose. About things changing. I know that better than anyone. I know that I have too much self pity but I just can't seem to stop feeling this anger. What you said about James and Sara, it's all true. And yet, I dunno, I feel so mixed up.'

'Because of your mum?'

He turns his face away and sighs. 'It's just … You don't know the whole story. You don't really understand why I'm so angry with Dad – he's been so good to you. How could you?'

It's my turn to rise onto an elbow. 'Tell me David. Tell me what happened.'

He looks up at me and a shadow crosses his eyes. 'She died in a car crash.'

Lifting a hand, he pushes a strand of hair from his forehead. The last trail of pink is fading from the window and the room is filled with the fire's dancing shadows.

'It was last April. Dad was driving and he was pissed. She'd warned him. Said she wouldn't go – not if he was going to drink.'

'Those scars on his face.'

'Yes.'

He reaches for my hand and grips it in his own. 'They were going to a dinner party with some of Mum's friends. She was always on at him not to drink but this night it was different. She wouldn't leave it alone, like she must have had some kind of premonition. There was a row. Dad went on and on about her having no faith in him and how he would never put her life at risk. She kept saying, "I know what you're like John, one glass is all it takes".

'What gets me – she was making such a fuss – y'know, it was strange, even for her. She said she wanted to go on her own, she didn't want him getting pissed and humiliating her. If it hadn't been for all those times I heard him promise he wouldn't drink I might not be so mad with him now.'

He falls silent, his eyes on the hawk as she preens herself sleepily above us. Then his bottom lip starts to tremble.

'The call came at midnight. They said there'd been an accident, my parents were in Salisbury Infirmary. It was serious … Audrey took me over. Sitting in her car, numb, and she was talking about cabbages. Fucking cabbages, can you believe it? Bloody Audrey, it's always talk and don't think, that'll be *her* epitaph.'

He turns his head towards me and hides his mouth in my neck. Again he's silent. I lift my hand and stroke his hair.

'So what happened at the hospital?'

'The doctor said the usual stuff: he was very sorry and all that; she'd been killed instantly, wouldn't have suffered …. Then Dad came out. His face was cut but he was fine. As soon as I saw the bastard I smelt it – his breath. It stank of whisky.'

He lifts himself forward and rests on his elbows. 'I mean *stank*. He was so arseholed he couldn't even walk straight. I went nuts. I punched him in the face and started kicking him. Can you believe it? I was so angry Nicola, so mad. They tried to hold me back. He kept telling me it wasn't his fault, "It's not my fault David, it's not my fault." That really drove me crazy. I mean, I could smell the stuff on him, for God's sake. Then the police showed up and carted him off to the station. They tested him and he was five times over the limit.'

He stares defiantly into the darkness.

'Audrey brought me back. She wanted to stay but I told her to go. I wanted to be on my own.'

He turns away from me as he lights a cigarette and takes fast, urgent drags, his face a mask of suppressed emotion.

'I couldn't live with him any more,' he continues. 'All I could think of was Mum, in the kitchen, earlier that evening, warning him not to drink, and him promising he wouldn't, the bastard….

'So I got some stuff together from my bedroom and moved in here. It took him days to find me. He thought I'd pissed off. He came up here eventually and started trying to talk to me – so I hit him again. After that I didn't open the door to anyone, didn't speak to anyone, not even Art. They all tried, Sara, James, Audrey. It was a beautiful thing when I realised it. If I went to the shop and Audrey started on me, I'd just walk out again. She soon learnt to keep her mouth shut.'

He reaches over me and grinds his cigarette against the ashtray. 'He only got a ban,' he adds bitterly. 'That's why Art drives him everywhere.'

I reach out and stroke his shoulder. 'What was she like?'

'Hmm?'

'Your mother.'

He turns to face me. 'We were very close. She, I dunno, thought I was her golden boy or something. She used to read a lot to me, poems and stuff – encouraged me to get into books. And she helped me with my painting, always telling me how talented I was when all Dad could do was crash around in some drunken haze. That's why I loved her so much. She was my ally, I could always talk to her about my problems. She was a very kind person – to everyone, not just me.'

He sighs and lies back in the bed. 'Her undoing really. If it wasn't for that she would never have stayed with Dad.'

'She never thought about leaving him?'

'No way. She wouldn't have done that. She might have left him but she'd never have left me. And it wasn't for a lack of choice. Men adored her. In the Swan you'd see their eyes following her. She kept her age so well, never lost her figure, or, I dunno, a kind of grace. Even Art was in love with her. Everyone was. She was beautiful, even to me, and I was her son.'

He turns his face towards me and there are tears in his eyes.

'Nicola, can we drop this now? This is the happiest day I've had since it happened and we've started talking about this shit.'

He pushes his wet cheek against mine. I feel his breath, warm against my ear. Then his hand clutches my hair and he pulls me against him.

The screams muddle their way into my unconscious. It's the dream but not the dream, somewhere there is the river, somewhere there is the grumbling water, freezing snow and the grey hides of the wolves, but this new sound, this sound of fear is unfamiliar to me. In the dream there's a new danger – an unknown strikes: a soft panicking mass, shrieks, cries, the thud of a body against wood and I became aware of frantically beating wings, of the hawk plunging from wall to wall. Raising my head, I think at first I am blind. A thick blackness coats and stings my eyes. It hangs before me like a heavy cape.

I shake David frantically. His body is soft and drowsy under my hands.

'David wake up!'

'Hmmm?'

'For God's sake David, the shed's on fire.'

Rancid smoke fills my nostrils.

'What?'

'The shed's on fire!'

I feel, because I cannot see, his body swing wildly. He jumps to his feet, his nails tearing my skin as he pulls me with him.

'The hose!'

He grips my arms as I stumble behind him, my sense of direction lost. The heat scorches my naked back. He's coughing and yanking at the door.

'I can't open it!'

'Shove it, kick it or something.'

Thick smoke fills our nostrils, choking us. I hear David wheezing and a terrible, rasping cough bursts from his chest.

'Open it, open it!'

I hammer his shoulders and he screams, then there's nothing but my own cries as the flames lick up against me.

'I'm burning I'm burning!'

There is a fumble of bodies. I feel David's hands around my wrists, pulling me from the heat. He shouts something, but I cannot hear his words. Suddenly we are sprawled in the clearing's dew-soaked grass. We lie still for several minutes, our naked bodies flung across the soft earth as we gulp the clear night air. I whisper a secret prayer of gratitude.

David springs to his feet and disappears. I turn my head and stare fearfully at the shed. The walls are not burning yet but everything inside, I realise, must be destroyed. The drawings, our clothes ….

David returns, the hose in his hands, water pouring from its end. He runs, naked, to the door, and begins spraying the bright flames.

'David, there's no point ….'

'My hawk's in there!'

I watch as great plumes of smoke bellow from the shed's mouth and rise against the dark treetops. David looks so pathetic, his trembling, naked body twisting to and fro in the doorway, but his strategy is working. I watch as the blaze is gradually reduced to small, scattered licks under the relentless stream of water until the last of the flame flickers and dies and we find ourselves in darkness.

'The lamp,' David mutters. He's inside the shed, searching frantically with his hands.

I approach the doorway.

'Jesus, all that and now I can't find a bloody light!'

'Your Zippo was by the fire.'

A minute later he has the paraffin lamp working. He lifts it and we survey the devastation around us. The mattress, the old red chairs, what's left of his canvasses. They're charred beyond recognition.

'Where is she? I can't see her.' His voice is hollow.

'Maybe she flew out.'

He glares at me, swinging the lamp around frantically.

'David!'

'What?' he snaps, but my tone has told him. He stops his dizzy circles and turns, his eyes full of dread.

I point to the corner of the room.

'There.'

He looks at me, and then to what is left of our bed. The charred blackness obscures nearly everything, but the lamp's light picks out the pale flecks of brown on the hawk's breast, the only colour left of her once beautiful plumage. David places the lamp on the floor and steps slowly towards her.

I watch silently as he kneels down and picks her up, gently, in his arms. His white nakedness contrasts with the black, charcoal neck as her head falls pathetically over his forearm, the beak dragging on the floor.

There is silence. Then his head falls back violently and the night is filled with a sobbing so wretched that even the trees seem to shiver in an unfelt wind.

Chapter Fourteen

So the door opened and for once it was us and no more. A small smile because you saw I had the cricket on, the dinner on, love waiting in a big hot pot, and you said – 'Got the message then, enjoying the game?'

Sarcasm – because you knew I hated cricket. The room was as sick as ever despite the flowers in your hand. Your presence, that cold thumb on my back, was there and that day, as usual, you were hostile. I looked up at what you were saying. Oven chips? No thanks, no matter how much you like the advert, it took me a long time to make this. Laughing, you said, 'You've got that look again' and I could have replied, 'Hey, you know this mask well – you put it on my face every time you're here.'

You just rubbed your hand through my hair and said, 'Let's skip the hot pot.'

You took me then, only it was me that was starving not you, tearing at your skin and devouring you. Not you. You were getting the best steaks, the Haute Cuisine, but like anyone of your class, you just couldn't give up the junk.

Turning away from me, my feet straddled over the couch, you picked up a tissue and mopped up the mess I'd made on you.

You got the booty. After that your eyes were bright, scheming. You were in a good mood, your head cocked, grinning like a school boy. You were feeling in control, weren't you? So we were watching cricket with the sound turned down and of course you were pretending you were interested. You reached down and patted the ash, it fell in a plump lump to the saucer. You hunched your shoulders and put a hand to your chin.

I concentrated on the whole of you and you knew I was waiting.

You talked about work.

Work? I didn't want to know about that other life – dumb faces and stupid drivers. I didn't want to know about salaries and how much Sheila got paid for going to that conference nobody wanted to know about. You talked about work and the seconds of our life were ticking away in a sobbing anti-climax.

What made you come into that house day after day and pretend the person you did not want to see did not exist?

'I don't know why I bother coming here.'

You knew why. You came and you denied that you were there; you came and you hid and you lied.

Up the hatch without a spanner. But there were no answers anyway, even if you did not offer them. Window talk, all of it. No, I would not play. I showed no expression. It was time you spoke, after all. I guessed what you were doing. It was you sitting in the Judas chair smugly breaking my heart.

Not me, my love,
not me.

PART TWO

It is early April and the forest's grass has grown lush and tall. I sit in the sunshine and watch David, his crouched body silhouetted against a backdrop of cloudless sky as he hammers a piece of felt onto the shed's roof. The clearing around us is now rich with anemones and ox slips, and the beeches and chestnuts, once so silently stern and naked, are resplendently fat with foliage.

I tilt my head back and close my eyes, letting myself enjoy the sun which warms my face. I concentrate on the low hum of insects in the grass and the sound of the forest's canopy which is alive with the chatter of birds. In the distance I can hear the low coo of a woodpigeon and from somewhere comes the intermittent drilling of a woodpecker.

I yawn and open my eyes. Rising wearily from the grass, I walk towards the shed where the rest of David's possessions are waiting and start shifting the charred remains of table and mattress, books and bedclothes onto a pile at the edge of the clearing. They make a sorry sight, the twisted, forlorn shapes of furniture David had used so well. By four o'clock I have finished. David climbs down from the roof and douses the heap with petrol. I step back as he sets light to it.

We stand at the edge of the fire and stare into its heart, watching with mutual exhaustion as the black smoke billows into the bright sky. Behind the fire, the treetops shimmer and melt as the rising wall of heat sends a flock of indignant rooks into the air.

'Well that's that then.' David says, his voice full of gloom.

'How long's it going to take?'

He shrugs. 'I dunno. I'm gonna have to put some supports in – it won't hold if there's a storm.'

'What about the furniture Audrey said we could have?'

'James is going to bring it up – when he's next home. But God knows if the shed'll be ready by then.'

We stand and watch the fire as evening begins to settle. The sky is turning a bluish-violet behind the dark tail of smoke and gnats form a cloud about our heads. From the distance comes the whir of a chainsaw.

'It's so peaceful here.'

David nods, then lifting a hand, gently strokes my hair.

'David?'

He stiffens. Morgan is trudging through the long grass towards us, his Barbour zipped up over flannel trousers which are pushed into the tops of black Wellingtons.

Morgan frowns as he removes his glasses.

'There's been a call from Caplan's. They want you to ring them back. Apparently it's urgent.'

David nods. 'All right. Thanks.'

Morgan watches his son turn and disappear into the blackened shed's doorway. Then he makes his way slowly around the fire until he reaches my side.

'You're getting there then?'

'Sort of, but it's hard work and we've still got loads to do.'

'Tell me Nicola,' he says, rubbing his chin, 'do you honestly think you'll be happy, living like this?'

'I'm sure I'll be fine Dr Morgan.'

A strong breeze carries the flames towards his feet and forces him to step back.

'What happened to 'John'? Sometimes I think you've changed since you've been with David. I rarely see you, and when I do you avoid talking to me. I thought we were chums.'

'I'm not trying to avoid you. We're busy, that's all.'

Morgan becomes silent, his face drawn. He turns to watch David climbing the ladder back onto the roof. Then he shakes his head. 'Make sure he rings Caplan's,' he says before heading towards the path.

As we walk down the overgrown lane back to the farm, I can feel David's tension at Morgan's intrusion. His face is set and his concentration is aimed at the tarmac beneath his feet.

'What's up?'

He shrugs but doesn't answer. I turn and concentrate on the fields around us. In the evening's fading light, they have lost their bleak colourlessness, becoming a landscape criss-crossed with folding greens and intermittent slanting golds.

'It won't be for much longer,' I say finally, my hand winding through the crook of his elbow.

'Won't it?' he says sharply. 'Since when did you become a builder?' Then he sighs, his fingers slipping onto mine and squeezing tightly. 'I'm sorry. It's just that I can't bear it much longer, being in that house. All his fucking pity, since the hawk died. I'm just sick of having to avoid his face every day, knowing he's desperate for the opportunity to put his case across.'

He reaches for his cigarettes. 'And then there's the anniversary.'

'What anniversary?'

'Next Thursday,' he says darkly, 'will be a year since Mum's death.' He looks ahead at the farm with a troubled expression. 'I wonder what Caplan's wants,' he mutters.

He showers as I make tea. Outside, the last strokes of daylight fade and the moon, high and creamy, sends a bright, ethereal light over the farm. I stand at the window and look at the stars.

David enters the kitchen, his face flushed from the shower. I make him some tea and then we both sit, mugs in hands, in silence. Upstairs, we can hear the familiar churn of Morgan's laser printer. David is exhausted, his eyes blinking heavily in an effort to stay awake. Outside, Art starts up the van, revving loudly as its wheels fight the pull of mud and gravel.

David yawns and rises to his feet. 'I'm going to call Caplan's.'

I pick up the mugs and rinse them under the tap, watching as Art struggles to get the van out of the mud.

From the sitting room comes David's voice, high-pitched, no longer tired. I turn, my ears keening to his words. Through the gap in the dining room door I see him standing quietly, his eyes on the telephone which he has placed back on its hook. He turns and catches my eye. For a second his face is blank, unrevealing. Then he grins and strides through the hall.

He throws me into the air.

'Yes!'

'David! What the …?'

He whirls me over his shoulders.

'Yes! Yes! Yes!'

A mug flies from my soapy hand and smashes against the dresser.

'For God's sake David!'

He sets me down and whoops, skipping around the kitchen like an Indian.

'What on earth is going on?'

Morgan stands at the door, his eyes moving disapprovingly from the scattered pieces of china to his son.

David's expression doesn't change with the appearance of his father. The younger man's face blazes with triumph. I reach forward, grabbing his arm and he immediately hugs me, his laughter filling the house. 'I've got an exhibition!'

He sits down in the rocking chair and flings back his head.

'Caplan, the old man, came down from London to see my stuff. They're giving me my own exhibition in Bristol. They do it every year – it's a promotional thing. They choose who they consider to be the best new artist around and show their stuff. If it's successful they shift it up to London.'

He drops his head back and stares up at the ceiling. His hands beat a fanfare on his thighs.

'When will this be?'

I look up at Morgan. He's staring at his son with a grave expression, as if he cannot believe the latter's good fortune.

David too, seems to hear the reservation in his father's voice. His face clouds as he turns and takes my hands.

'In four weeks.'

'Hence the urgency?'

David nods. 'Can you believe it?' he exclaims. 'I'm a real painter. It's my profession. People will take me seriously. I didn't realise how big Caplan's is, they have shops all over the place.'

Then his tone changes to one of concern. 'It'll hold up work on the shed of course. You don't mind, do you?'

I shake my head and grip his hands fiercely.

Noticing the suppressed communication between us, Morgan tactfully moves toward the stairs. He pauses at their foot and turns back towards us.

'David?'

David lifts his head.

'May would have been proud of you.'

As David stares at his father, there's a sudden tension in the air. As usual, the mention of his mother's name is like somebody lighting a fuse. His hands stiffen over mine and the smile fades from his face. 'If she was still alive,' he mutters.

A shadow passes over Morgan's face. He remains at the bottom of the stairs, unable to draw himself away. David glances at him, then stares ahead into space.

'I wish you would listen,' Morgan says after a pause. 'You're so wrong.'

His son rises from the chair with determination.

'For God's sake. It wasn't my fault, it was an ….'

'Shut the fuck up!'

Then he's gone, the door slamming behind him.

Morgan sighs, his eyes watching the chair which still rocks from his son's violent departure. We listen to David's footsteps stamping furiously down the drive.

'If he knew,' Morgan says quietly, 'none of this would be happening. Why won't he listen?'

I rest my hand on the Aga's warm rail.

'I so badly want to talk to him,' he continues. 'Just a few sentences could change all this. We've all tried: me, James, Audrey. He pushes us all away. Even Art – and he's know him half his life. If he doesn't trust Art then who can he trust?'

He breaks off as outside, Art starts the van's engine. I turn my face to the window and listen to the wheels spinning.

'I wish I could tell you what happened, Nicola, but it would turn him against you too if he saw you as part of this great conspiracy. That's why I'd rather you didn't know. If you knew, you would feel forced to tell him.'

I move towards the door.

'Where are you going?' he asks.

'To find him. I'm worried he's going to do another bunk.'

'I don't think so, Nicola.'

But I'm already closing the door and stepping out into the night. I stand there, staring into the dark and looking for a sign of David. Then I start to walk.

The first thing I pass is Art's van, still stranded in the mud under the milky light of the moon. There's no sign of its driver. Beyond it the pale fields merge with a sky full of stars.

The ground is soft under my feet and a cool breeze lifts my hair – yet I have a sudden prickly feeling, as if something is not quite right. I look around but see only the single light of Morgan's kitchen window following my back like an unblinking eye. I look for the shape of Morgan's head watching me through the window, but there is nothing.

A strange silence settles over the land, an omnipresence. Although the moon is high and the air warm, a feeling of foreboding pulses in the darkness. Shadows seem to shudder in the corner of my eye and the breeze pauses around me with a disarming hush.

A man comes from the barns and walks slowly in my direction. He holds something in his hand.

But the figure is not David. He looms toward me with his eyes to the ground, unaware of my presence. The thing he holds is a sack, taken from the hay barn.

'Art?'

He comes to a halt a few feet away, ghostly in the moonlight.

'Lookin' for David?'

I nod.

'Went o'er the fields. Rowing' with 'is dad again I s'pose?'

'Yes.'

He shrugs. 'Someone should put a stop to it. None of my business mind but that lad deserves 'is ears boxin'.'

He pauses. 'Got to sort this van. Put this sack under the wheel – maybe get some grip.' He starts toward the house. I watch his back, and then, before I know it, call his name. He comes to a halt and turns towards me, his expression suspicious.

'Art,' I say quietly, 'do you remember what you said in the barn that day? You said Morgan had ideas for me. And you said you would tell me if you were right.'

He looks at me wordlessly, his eyelids flickering.

'It was about David wasn't it? You thought Morgan was using me to reach him.'

Art lifts the sack over his shoulder.

'Well? – you said you would tell me if you were right.'

'Not usin' you,' he murmurs finally. ''Ee wanted you to be David's friend – that's all. Reckon 'ee's worried now – seein' 'ow quickly the lad's got smitten.'

He takes a step toward the van, then pauses, his breath rising in a cloud of condensation.

'And you – are you worried?'

''Bout David? No. 'Ee's a grown up, though you wouldn't know it 'alf the time.'

'But you don't like me, do you? You never have. Not really.'

He regards me carefully from under his cap. In the moonlight his pale face looks more like wax than flesh and blood.

'It's not for me to be telling you this,' he says finally. 'But you just remember 'ow well John's treated you. There's people in the village not 'appy 'bout you livin' off 'is goodwill.'

'Meaning Audrey Burrows.'

'Meaning no names. Just you remember, that's all.'

He goes off in the direction of the van, his shoulders hunched. In the darkness he looks like a man of sixty. I watch his departing figure and feel a surge of anger rising inside me.

I do not want to go over the fields in search of David, neither do I want to return to the house. The night and Art's words have unsettled me. As I move toward the barns I feel as if I'm caught in a triangle of dark forces. It's as if the strange presence still follows, grows closer. From inside the wooden buildings comes the stamping of hooves, a violent snort. The animals, too, sound alarmed, as if something or someone has disturbed them.

I turn back towards the house. Even Morgan's company is preferable to this all-consuming sense of being judged by another force, a force much more sinister than anything that Art can throw at me.

Morgan sits in the rocking chair, waiting, his face tired.

'He'll come back.'

I lean against the Aga. 'I know.'

He rises from the chair and, moving to the Aga, lifts the scuttle to shunt coal into the fire. Closing the stove door, he stands up and turns to face me.

'Nicola?' he says. 'What's up? You look terrible.'

'It's nothing. I'm fine.'

'Nothing? You look as mad as hell.'

I sit down at the table, my mind churning over Art's words. Then I raise my head and look doubtfully at Morgan. 'Dr Morgan, if I ask you something, will you tell me the truth?'

He smiles. 'Well, I can try.'

'It's just that ....' I glance down at my hands. 'I wonder sometimes if you think I'm using you.'

Immediately his eyes narrow and his mouth purses. 'Who have you been talking to?'

I shake my head and look down. 'No one. It's just that ... you've always been so good to me ... I have no way to repay you.'

He moves towards me and places a hand, gently, on my shoulder. 'I don't think you're using me Nicola. Wanting to live in that awful shack – it's not the life most people would choose. And look at what you've done for David – in that sense you've already paid me back tenfold. No, if you must know, the thing that concerns me about you is your past – or the lack of it. I still know nothing about you and that worries me, especially as you've become so involved with my son. I don't understand why you're so secretive about this ex. Is he looking for you?'

I look at the ground and don't reply.

'You see. How can I *not* be worried when you won't answer such a simple question? What are you hiding Nicola? Are you worried this man's going to find ....'

We jump as the door bursts open and David staggers in. His jeans and jumper, clean on earlier, are splattered with mud and grass. His eyes swing wildly round the room.

He comes to a halt, his hands finding the table edge and clutching it. His face, even under the warmth of the side lamp, is drained of colour.

'David?' I say.

Morgan and I look at each other, our conversation forgotten. David swings round at the sound of my voice, then moves to the door. He yanks it opens and his eyes search the darkness.

'David,' his father mutters, 'what the …?'

David slams the door shut, turning the large, iron key with shaking hands. 'I was going to the river,' he gasps. 'To the bridge. There was a terrible noise ….' He breaks off, his breath coming fast. 'A terrible noise,' he repeats.

'What kind of noise?' Morgan asks.

But David shakes his head. He sits down at the table and lets his face fall into his hands. 'Screaming,' he mutters, 'like somebody or something screaming. It was so loud.'

I step towards him.

'Maybe it was the wind,' Morgan suggests.

'That wasn't wind,' his son mutters into his palms. 'That was no way wind.'

He is silent, his breathing beginning to calm. Morgan stands up and switches on the main strip light, then looks at the ghost-like face of his son. David's skin is drawn tight across his cheekbones, his eyes red from the cold night air.

Morgan sits down opposite. 'You think someone was there?'

David raises his head and glares at Morgan.

'There must have been, but that's the point. I couldn't see anyone. I couldn't see anything. There was this weird darkness – yet it's almost a full moon.'

132

I stand up and move over to David, my hand resting lightly on his shoulder.

'It wasn't a person,' he mutters. 'But it was real – whatever it was.' Some colour has come back into his cheeks as his frustration with Morgan overtakes his panic.

'You don't believe me do you? You're all wound up with your doctor's logical shit.'

Morgan sighs. 'I do believe you David. Nicola and I heard a similar sound once. But it was a storm, that was all.'

I've been thinking the same thing. That night, a blackthorn winter – the wind screaming; my dreams; the cries in my head; the eerie presence which had driven me back to this house just half an hour ago.

David turns to me. 'There's some whisky in my coat, in the utility room. Can you get it?'

I return to find them sitting in silence. Morgan's eyes rest on his son, more concerned with David than the terrible noise. I pour a stiff measure into a glass and pass it to the younger man. He reaches for it blindly.

'It started like … like a kind of whistling,' David mutters. 'Then it turned into, I dunno, a scream – it sounded like it was coming from the river. I was walking through the lower field, thinking about you. Thinking about us. Then … it was terrible, like someone being tortured. Like – I don't know – the worst thing in the world, the thing you never ever want to hear.'

He lifts the glass to his lips, and holds it there, his eyes staring over its rim ahead into emptiness. Then he knocks the whisky back in one.

Chapter Sixteen

In the following days, I begin to see a growing disturbance in David. On the outside he still appears motivated, still busily occupied with the building of the shed and preparing for the exhibition. But the episode at the river has left a shadow over his fragile, over-sensitive view of life. He cannot help but see it as some kind of dreadful omen.

'You don't understand because you weren't there,' he snaps one night, after waking up in a pool of sweat. 'I can't get it out of my head. I keep hearing it. I keep *dreaming* about it. All the time.'

But it's Morgan who enlightens me to the real source of David's trauma. 'He's got it all muddled in his head,' Morgan remarks one morning when we're alone. 'He's stressed and it's leading to bad dreams. He's focusing on that night but that's not what's really winding him up. It's Thursday he's really thinking about – the anniversary of May's death.'

As the days go by, David's moodiness and intractability becomes ever more apparent. Though he paints around the clock, he barely mentions the exhibition. He's distracted, aloof, his thoughts far away. So I'm not surprised, when the dreaded day finally arrives, to wake up alone, staring through the window at a sky which is grey and overcast after weeks of brilliant sunshine.

'Where's David?'

I stand with my chin pressed against the edge of Morgan's office door. Morgan sits with his back to me, drawing quietly on a cigarette.

'I woke up and he was gone.'

He turns round in the chair, his face heavy with fatigue. Over his shoulder I can see the rain batter the window panes.

'He'll want to be alone today, Nicola.'

'I know. I just wondered. It's pouring with rain and I'm worried he's out in it somewhere.'

Morgan rubs the end of a pen against his chin. His eyes look strained and I realise that this day is hitting him hard too. He rises from the chair and moves towards me.

'I'm sure he can look after himself Nicola. Let him be.'

'I know, but he was in such a state last night. All of yesterday. He wouldn't speak to me.'

'It's his way. Give him his space.'

I grit my teeth and nod. I expect him to return to his work, but instead he follows me. We walk down the stone steps side by side and enter the dismally-lit kitchen.

Outside the rain-splattered window, the barns shiver and shimmer and the wind, as if summoned by some reproachful God, stirs threateningly.

Morgan places a mug of coffee before me and sits down wearily. 'Art's driving me to Morton. You want anything?'

I shake my head.

'Thought I'd have a chat with Audrey,' he continues, 'James is down in a fortnight. We could get that furniture up.'

He swallows his coffee quickly and rises as if to go. Then he pauses. 'Has all this interfered with his painting?'

I shrug. 'Well he's not satisfied with his work at the moment, I know that much. But I don't know if it's because of today or pressure from the exhibition.'

He sighs. 'It's really something, to get that show. And if he sells some paintings, well, maybe earning some real money'll encourage him to lead a normal life like James – instead of this hand-to-mouth existence.'

'David will never lead a normal life,' I say.

Morgan stands up and puts his hand on my shoulder before moving away towards the utility room.

135

He returns with his Barbour over his arm and hovers as he searches in its pockets for his car keys.

'I'll see you later then.'

I nod and put down my coffee.

'You won't want to know him today Nicola. He'll be a wreck.'

'I know.'

After he's gone, I sit and watch the rain weave its way down the window pane and soak the crumbling sill. Deliberating between going to find David and staying in the dry, I pad around the house wearily as morning turns into afternoon and there's still no sign of him. The weather is turning from bad to worse – heavy storm clouds gather in a mass over the horizon until the whole sky has turned a thunderous black.

I wonder if David is out in this, and what the consequences of that might be. He will not care about anything today. I look at the pouring rain and think of the oncoming exhibition. A nasty premonition haunts me, but I remember Morgan's warning and fight the urge to go out.

But when another hour has ticked by and there's still no sign of him, I pick up a macintosh and walk determinedly into the rain. I know it's foolish. Even if my guess is correct I'll be soaked through by the time I reach the shed. And if he's there, what can I do? I have felt this coming for the past week. It has been in every word spoken to Morgan, every moment he has fought to spend alone. My presence will be of no comfort today – yet still I walk, ignoring my better judgement.

I battle toward the stile, bowing my head as the suffocating water hits me in sheets and thick tails of dripping hair plaster my face, which is twisted sideways into my hood. Staring with squinting eyes at the flooded tarmac beneath me, I feel the water seep into my boots, which are now battered and full of holes from constant exposure to the farm's mud and gravel.

The wind tears through the trees and in its echo I suddenly hear the whistling coming from the depths of the forest. As I listen, my eyes screwed against the stinging rain, I imagine it moving through the trees, its invisible feet pounding the mud. My heart rips, I rush forward, pushing the hair from my face.

I climb the path hurriedly, fighting to escape the terrible sound, my feet sliding wildly in the waterlogged ground as I grapple for branches to help me balance. Over my head I hear the first grumble of thunder and I force myself on, my fingers grabbing at twigs and thorns which rip flesh from under my knuckles. The ghostly whistle gradually fades and dies.

At the same time, and with a deep sigh of relief, I see him, a blurred figure in the rain. He's crouched outside the shed staring dismally at the ground, a bottle of whisky pressed to his mouth.

He shifts slightly, hearing my footsteps, and raises his eyes to meet mine.

A glaze of muddy water coats his face, staining his cheeks. His pale jumper and jeans are soaked, sticking to his body like glue and his dark head slumps forward over his chest as water drips from his hair and courses down his neck.

He's drunk. His skin is sanguine and his squinting, bloodshot eyes peer dully into mine.

'David?'

Numerous cigarette butts litter the grass at his feet. He's smoking now, dragging absently on a damp Camel between slugs of whisky.

He lifts an unsteady arm and hold the bottle towards me.

'No, thanks.'

I squat down beside him on the west grass and put my hand on his shoulder, but he shakes his head and looks at the ground. Long strands of hair cling to his face.

'Wanted to be alone.'

I reach out a hand and touch his shoulder. He pitches forward, his forehead pressed into his hands.

'Leave me alone.'

'I'm worried about you.'

'I'll be okay.'

'You should come home.'

'No.'

'David, you must. It's pissing down. You'll get ill. What about the exhibition – do you want to blow that?'

He shifts violently away from me, his fingers ploughing into the mud as he turns his face toward the forest.

I watch him doubtfully from under the coat's dripping hood. I have never seen him like this before, so helpless, so out of control. A whole year has passed since his mother's death and still he's reduced to this.

I lean a wet hand against the shed and push myself up. He cowers, his shoulders narrowing. With his right hand he gropes for the whisky bottle.

'This is stupid David. You look like a ….'

'I'm just drunk,' he mumbles. 'I'm drunk. Can't you leave it?'

A crash of thunder interrupts him. He looks up at the sky, then back to the dense forest. I shiver, not knowing what to do. Rain seeps through the thick macintosh. I feel my shirt collar sticking to my neck.

'This time,' he mutters, 'this time she was in the garden.'

'This time?'

'The weather was good. Sunshine. She was singing.'

'You mean this time last year?'

'That Joplin song, y'know. *Summertime*. Said it was the first real day of spring.'

He breaks off and pushes the end of his cigarette into the sodden ground, turning it slowly.

'Ten hours later she was dead.'

He lets himself fall back heavily, his head pressed into his arms as he curls up like a foetus. I reach over and take the bottle from his hand then screw the lid back on tightly. The shed door swings heavily in the wind and the soaking grass quivers. I set the bottle down beside him and tug gently on his coat sleeve. But he refuses to move, his body a dead weight. I sit for some minutes then tug again.

'David, please, I can't leave you here. Please come home.'

'Can't.'

'Yes you can.'

I shove him into a sitting position. But his head rolls on his shoulders and his eyes remain shut.

'David!'

He doesn't stir. I glance around the clearing with frustration before my eyes spot the hose, still lying on the grass where it was discarded on the night of the fire.

I pick up its end and walk through the long grass, following its meandering path to the tap, under a large beech tree. I turn it on and return to David, who has not moved, his body sprawled in the soaking grass. I survey him for a second or two with pity, then lift the hose and shoot a stream of water over his face and chest.

'*What the ...!*'

'Get up, or I'll do it again.'

He presses an arm over his face and looks up at me like a wounded animal gazing at its trapper.

'I said, get up!'

'Nicky please ....'

I send him another shot of water.

'Fucking hell! Leave me alone will you?'

'C'mon David. I'm taking you home.'

He rolls onto his knees, his eyes half-closed. I reach down and grasp his arm. He climbs to his feet unsteadily, his weight falling against me. I shower his head with the hose and he yells, staggering backward.

'Now stay like that while I turn this thing off.'

When I return, he's leaning heavily against the shed, his wet head hanging low. I pull one of his dripping arms around my shoulders and half-carry him toward the track.

We negotiate the stile. He crashes into it, his eyes still half-shut. He hangs there while I put his hands on the top bar and lift his foot onto the muddy step. He heaves himself upward, loses his balance, and falls with a crash onto the road's grass verge.

He rises to his feet with an angry shake of his head.

'You should have left me there. Don't you understand?'

I push him forward. 'What if it had been me David? You would never have left me.'

He raises two wobbly hands, staggering along the road like a blind man. I hear the whistling sound, closer this time – a thin, pitiful wailing on the late afternoon air.

I shiver, and walk faster, watching David to see if he hears it too, but he staggers on silently, his eyes blazing with fury, and shows no sign of hearing anything. It hangs in the distance, growing fainter as we make our way towards the farm. When we reach the drive it has gone, withdrawing like an animal giving up on its prey. David stumbles over the potholes, swearing loudly. I reach out to take his arm but he yanks it away.

'I *can* walk you know.'

'For God's sake David.'

'If you'd just fucking well left me alone ….'

We draw up to the house and he falls heavily against the porch door as he fiddles with the latch. I turn and search the horizon, my ears straining for the sound.

Opening the door, the first thing we see is Morgan, sitting in the rocking chair with *The Times* on his knee. He's not reading and the room is full of cigarette smoke. He raises his head in annoyance.

'Nicola, I said to leave ....' But then he breaks off, watching his son, as David, dripping wet and red-eyed, half falls into the room and slumps against a wall. The two men face each other without speaking.

'He's drunk,' I announce. 'I couldn't leave him there could I? not in this weather. I'll get him into a hot bath.'

'Best place for him,' remarks his father.

David doesn't move. He glares at Morgan through his muddy fringe and staggers toward the table, crashing hard against one of the chairs.

'David, please. Come upstairs.'

'Feeling *good* today, are we Dad?'

He's leaning heavily against the back of the chair. It begins to wobble under his weight.

'Go with Nicola,' Morgan says quietly, still with the same unwavering glare.

I put a hand on David's shoulder. 'Do as he says David.'

He turns round and gives me such a look of scorching hate that I step back.

'Who are you?' he says. 'My mother?' He lurches toward me and grabs my arm. 'I hope you don't think you're my mother. Because my mother's dead.'

'David, please.'

'She's dead.'

He turns to face his father, his face hot with loathing.

'That stupid fuck over there. He murdered her. She told him but he wouldn't listen, would he? Never were much good at listening were you, you stupid fucking bastard ...?'

'That's enough David.'

'Wadaya mean, "that's enough"? Of course it isn't enough. I haven't even started yet you stupid shit.'

His father stands up and faces his son with a cold look.

'You don't know what you're talking about.'

'I don't know what I'm talking about? She was my mother, for God's sake. You killed her. You went out and you got pissed, even though she'd told you a thousand times not to do it. No you wouldn't listen, would you? Never did when it came to the booze. Always *you, you, you.*'

'I didn't kill her.'

The fist shoots out. It happens so quickly that I don't see it until it makes contact with Morgan's nose. There's a resounding crack of bone on bone and he crashes to the ground, his head smacking against the rocking chair which tips back and forward over him as he lies without moving. Blood trickles across his ear onto the cold brick floor beneath.

I feel dazed.

'Don't lie to me! Don't lie to me you bastard. How can you fucking well stand there and say that?'

David yanks his arm from my grip and stands over his father. His breath comes in short gasps. Morgan's eyes are open and he looks blearily up at his son. Blood pours from his nostrils as his eyes travel weakly over David's face, then mine.

'For God's sake David, you could have killed him!' I shout.

David turns, his face full of fury, and I flinch, believing he will hit me too. But he simply glares and turns back to his father who is climbing dazedly to his feet, his hands gripping the dresser.

'How can you just carry on,' David continues, 'knowing what you've done? How can you just live this boring, empty, meaningless life? You're a laughing stock, don't you know that?

142

Everyone in the fucking village … the way they talk. Do you know how that makes me feel?'

Morgan steadies himself. There's no fear, only weariness and defeat in his face. I leave the room quickly and return with some tissue.

I pull on David's arm and at the same time the sight of the blood, still oozing from Morgan's nose, appears to subdue him. He steps backwards, falling against me, and I lower him into one of the kitchen chairs. He looks at his father, his head swaying.

'You never learn do you? You always have to ….'

The sound of footsteps interrupts him. I turn and look out of the window to see Art struggling toward the house, carrying a hammer, his face bowed against the rain. He pauses at his van, dropping the hammer onto a front seat, and makes his way towards the front door.

David stiffens as the farmhand enters the kitchen, water pouring from his cap. He nods to us.

'Got most of it done, John, still a problem with the ….'

The sight of Morgan's bloody face stops his words. At the same time, Morgan groans loudly. Art glances at him, then towards David. The farmhand's lips tighten.

'When you goin' to grow up?'

David shifts uncomfortably and attempts to rise to his feet. But suddenly Art is above him, his powerful arms, strengthened by years of farm work, holding him down.

Morgan shakes his head and murmurs, 'Leave him Art.'

But Art ignores him. He stares coldly at David. ''Oo do you think you are, 'itting a man twice your age? 'Ow long's this gonna go on? What you stayin' 'ere for if this is the way you're gonna repay 'im?'

David struggles hard under his grip. 'You know the fucking score Art, you know ….'

'I know the score,' Art shouts. 'But you don't. All this mopin', this temper. Someone should bloody well teach you a lesson.'

Morgan is trying to staunch the bleeding, tilting his head and exerting pressure over the bridge of his nose. Outside the storm still rages, tearing over the house and farm. The gale punishes the window frames and a tile crashes from the roof.

David glowers, his body still trapped under Art's hands as Morgan sits apart from us, dabbing quietly at his nose as the bleeding begins to subside. Art looks at him, his face still hot with anger. He looks down at David.

'Your father's got something to tell you.'

Morgan looks at Art with alarm.

'You tell 'im John,' Art says coldly. 'Or I'm off this farm for good. I've 'ad enough. I mean it. There's plenty other places I can work. I'm not puttin' up with this any more. If May could've seen this ....'

Morgan winces.

'She wouldn't 'ave stood for this. I always say it's not my business John. But it is my business. I'm piggy-in-the-middle 'ere.'

Morgan lifts the tissue to his nose and studies the drying blood. He sighs.

'Alright Art, let's try it your way.'

David heaves himself violently against Art and his shouting fills the room. 'You can't, you bastards! You can't make me listen, you can't!'

Art shoves him roughly against the dresser, pinning both wrists behind him. 'Your father's got somethin' to tell you. So you will bloody well shut up or I won't be responsible for what I'll do to you.'

He clenches a fist against David's head and I see a flicker of fear in David's expression.

'David,' Morgan says suddenly. 'Do you remember a man called Kyle McLaughlin?'

David looks away.

'Do you remember him? He was our solicitor.'

The younger man shakes his head violently.

'Would you tell him please, Art?'

Art's eyes flit between Morgan and his son. Morgan's face remains expressionless, David's head is bowed.

'Wasn't your dad's fault what 'appened,' Art growls. His fingers tighten on David's shoulders. 'McLaughlin's in prison. For killin' Mrs Morgan.'

David immediately begins to struggle, shifting his body in a violent attempt to throw Art off, but once more the farmhand's hands anticipate him.

'You are bloody well goin' to listen,' Art mutters, his breath coming in short bursts. Nobody speaks. David's brow furrows and I see him begin to consider Art's words. His expression becomes sober and, to my surprise, he stops struggling.

Art turns to Morgan. 'You tell 'im the rest, John.'

'No.' David raises his head stiffly and looks at the farmhand. 'You tell me. If I *have* to listen to this shit then I'd rather not hear it from his lying mouth.'

Art looks at Morgan. He nods.

'Your dad and Mrs Morgan were stopped at a junction,' the farmhand continues. 'The A424 outside Salisbury. They was lookin' at a map. There were some problems gettin' 'ome cos the Salisbury road were closed an' they 'ad to find another way.' He pauses. 'An' McLaughlin drove into 'em, fast like … deliberate. Drove into the front of the car, but 'ee mainly 'it Mrs Morgan's side. They didn't stand a chance like, bein' stopped an' that, both lookin' at the map.'

He looks over at Morgan who bows his head.

'Police picked 'im up few hours later. 'Ee was drunk as a skunk.'

'He went down for manslaughter,' Morgan finishes gently. He looks at the younger man. 'The whisky you smelt on my breath David ...,' he continues quietly. 'I kept my promise to your mother. I didn't drink at the party. I drank after the crash. I had a bottle in the back of the car.'

The temper has drained from David's face. He stares ahead in a kind of stupor. 'I don't believe it,' he mutters, his voice flat. He rises slowly to his feet, his hand gripping the table for support. Art retreats but his body remains braced. 'I don't believe it. He had no reason.'

Morgan lowers his head and doesn't answer.

'Well? Tell me, Art. Give me one good reason.'

Art shakes his head. David whirls around and looks at me. I shrug helplessly. He turns back to his father.

'I don't believe it. Even if he's in prison. He had no reason ... but you did, you were pissed. I don't care what you say.'

'He did have a reason,' Morgan says quietly. 'Of a sort.'

His father shakes his head and moves towards his son. Morgan, to my astonishment, starts to cry.

David is trembling. 'Well, what was it? Why would he kill her? Tell me, for God's sake. You've waited long enough.'

He's still angry, he shows no sympathy with his father's tears but his voice jerks Morgan out of his grief. Morgan looks up at David and his ageing eyes are red. He extends a shaking arm forward and clasps his son's shoulder. David flinches but Morgan reaches up and knots his other hand into his son's mud-splattered hair. He pulls his son's head hard against the shoulder of his shirt. David's shocked face stares at me over Morgan's arm as his father begins to rock back and forward, his wretched sobs filling the room.

Art shifts, his eyes flickering up awkwardly, then lowering again. I look into Morgan's face. He meets my gaze through his tears and a final understanding is shared.

I circle round them until I'm looking at David over Morgan's shoulder. I lift my hand to stroke his chin. At the same time Morgan says, 'He was her lover, David, that's why.'

'You see, in a way it was *my* fault. I was such a rotten husband to May – how could I blame her for having an affair?'

We are sitting in Morgan's small living room. David leans forward and stares vacantly into the flames of a newly-built fire. The effects of the whisky are subsiding and the beginnings of a fearsome hangover weigh heavily on his eyelids.

His face no longer wears its usual weaponry. No anger lurks there, no vitriol. At this moment he looks disturbingly like his father, weary and defeated, shoulders bowed and his mouth grim.

In the other corner of the room, withdrawn from us now, sits Art. He has removed his cap, revealing a large bald patch on the crown of his head. His eyes too are lowered but his gaze flickers from side to side. Outside, a moonless night has claimed the land. The wind blasts and rain slams against the windows.

Morgan sits in the armchair, his purpling nose crusted with drying blood. A heavy silence ensues, the three men buried in their own thoughts as the fire throws patterns on their faces.

Eventually Morgan raises his head. Polishing his glasses absently on his sweater, he looks at his son.

'I don't know all the details,' he says. 'And I don't want to. The farm's books were in a mess – down to me of course. One of our customers had put in a large order which I forgot to note. He lost money and took us to court, so May decided we needed a solicitor.'

He puts his glasses back on and stares into the flames. He's silent for a while, his face contemplative. Then he sighs. 'So she got in touch with Kyle McLaughlin.'

Shadows play across the room's fading walls. I see patterns, dark shapes pirouetting like exhausted dancers. My eyes skirt the dusty mantelpiece, the unswept piles of ash around the hearth.

But it's not the dust, nor the decay, which most strikes me now, it's the feeling of tiredness in this house, of weight.

'I don't know when it turned into something else,' Morgan continues. 'He worked for us for around a year. It hadn't been going on all that long, maybe a couple of months. But they became obsessed with each other.'

'And you didn't know?' I ask gently.

He sighs. 'I didn't know about it for sure, not until after the crash. But I suspected something. She was always going to Salisbury on some pretext or other. I even accused her of it, but she always denied it.'

David presses his face into his hands. 'I remember.'

'And you blamed the rows on me.'

'No, I mean I remember all those visits she made.'

Morgan nods and stands up. He moves over to the window and pulls back the faded material. He watches the rain for a while then takes out a handkerchief and blows his nose.

'If it wasn't for me she would never have met him. I was giving her no attention and she was still a very beautiful woman. Along came McLaughlin – a spoilt and ruthless man. He knew what he wanted; he didn't like to be denied.'

In the far corner Art shifts uncomfortably. Morgan sighs, his hands dropping the curtain. 'The night she died,' he says softly, 'she didn't want me to go to that party. You must remember.' He turns to face his son. 'We had a big fight about my drinking. She nagged me for hours.'

David nods blindly. I remember him telling me of the awful vividness of this particular memory, his mother pleading and pleading with Morgan not to drink.

'It was manipulation David. It was his housewarming party, in the house that he'd bought for *them* to live in. That's why she didn't want me to go. The drinking just gave her an excuse. She'd arranged to get a taxi over and supposedly stay the night at Angela's. But I changed my mind. She didn't expect that because I never went to that kind of thing – partly because I hate parties, but mainly because I couldn't drink. That night I'd made up my mind. I'd decided that just for once I'd control myself for her sake, so that *she* could have a good time without the drag of having to stay over at someone's house.

'Well, he was there, waiting for her – and none too pleased when I showed up. According to Angela, who was in on the whole thing, there was a row; he tried to force an ultimatum – for her to tell me there and then what was going on. Of course she couldn't have done that, not in the middle of a party. But then, he was not a reasonable man.'

Morgan turns back to the window. 'Angela said May told him to get lost and that was what blew it. Personally I think she was scared – of him, of me, of the whole situation she'd got herself into. She couldn't handle it. So we left, and he got drunk – very drunk. He got into a jealous rage and took after us in his car. I didn't know any of this at the time except May wanted to go and she was in a mood. It's ironic though ....'

He looks at his hands, as if momentarily forgetting us. 'I remember watching him at the party. By then I knew what he was, and I suppose that deep inside I had guessed about the affair because she never said that McLaughlin would be there, let alone that it was his party. He was a lot younger than May, a lot younger – that doesn't make me feel very good either. Full of himself, ambitious. And though I hate to say it, I could see he was very handsome, very charming.'

He becomes silent and looks out of the window once more. The mop of silver hair falls lankly over his furrowed brow.

'He only got five years,' he says bitterly. 'And now they've sent him to Chapelton Open Prison. He's got satellite TV, the works. What kind of world do we live in where justice takes this form?'

The rhetorical question is followed by more silence. I look at the photograph of May Morgan, that enigmatic smile, those dark, liquid eyes.

'They were planning to live together,' Morgan continues. 'I think that's why the row hit him so hard, why he reacted so violently – he'd bought that place for them. He thought she was bottling out. Of course he didn't know May like we did. He pushed her into a corner, that's all. No doubt if he'd left her alone they would have made it up. May would never have let somebody invest that amount of time in her unless she was serious. But he couldn't see that. All he could see was her snubbing him at the party he was holding for her – and in front of their friends.'

Morgan closes the curtain and returns to his chair. His face is cool and grave. Again he seeks his son's eyes but David lowers them and turns his face away.

'I'm not sorry for the things I've said, Dad.' David speaks quietly, but in a cutting tone I've never heard before. 'Despite everything you've told me. You're still a drunk, you still gave me a miserable childhood. There's nothing you can do or say which will make up for that.'

His father grimaces. 'David, I know. But it's like a hammer, alcoholism. You think you're in control until it hits you over the back of the head. By the time I realised I had a problem it was too late. Too late for May anyway. You were always right about that.

'I knew what a terrible father I was being, and husband. But I didn't know how to stop it. I don't know David, because I've spent so little time with you. If you have any idea what it's like to feel like you're about to go to pieces, that's how I felt when I couldn't drink. That fear was worse than the fear of losing my family. It's impossible to explain unless you've been through it.

Don't you understand? It's an illness. I was sick and I didn't know how to help myself.

'After your mother died, I really felt I had nothing to live for. I'd lost my wife, my son, my job. For a while I did nothing, I just languished in my own self-pity. Then I started to realise. It was the day that I went up to the shed and you hit me – before I'd had a chance to explain.'

He removes his glasses once again and starts polishing them with the edge of his pullover. 'That terrible day …. Leaving the shed with a bloody nose and walking back through the forest, I realised I really did have nothing to live for. Even my own son didn't want to know me. I think it was at that moment, that small silent moment standing alone outside your shed, that I saw everything had been a lie, that I was not in control of my drinking and had not been for a very long time … May's affair, her death. Your hitting me ….'

David glances at his father, then looks down again.

'And so I saw that if I had to live, if I were to do anything that could possibly right any of those wrongs, I also had to be punished, and the only way to do that was to tackle the devil which had indirectly ruined my family. There was one thing left in my grasp, one thing I could take control of. It would never bring back the past but it was, perhaps, one small way of punishing myself, of appeasing my pathetic, impotent conscience. So I stopped drinking.'

David leans forward and his mouth tightens. 'So easy. After all those years.'

'No David, it wasn't easy. They put me on drugs while I dried out. It wasn't a pleasant experience. Even now I still crave a drink. Don't let that happen to you. Don't get cursed by this thing because it will destroy everything you have. Do you want to lose Nicola the way I lost May?'

David opens his mouth but Morgan lifts a finger. 'I don't mean the crash, I mean before the crash. Do you want to alienate her, make her feel useless, incapable of helping? You know how my drinking made May feel, do you want Nicola to go through the same thing?'

'I haven't made her ....'

'You have today. Would you have spoken to her like you did earlier if you hadn't been drinking? Would you have been violent? Of course you wouldn't. Could she take this kind of behaviour day after day? Would you want her to?'

'She doesn't ....'

'She might. How do you know? Wouldn't you take every step to prevent it? Isn't it better to stop now, before it really gets you? Think ahead David. Alcoholism is often hereditary. Your life is going somewhere now. Please don't wreck it the way I wrecked mine.'

David averts his face again. He takes a deep breath and his hands are trembling.

'I still don't think I'll ever forgive you, Dad' he says finally. 'I don't even know if I want to.' His head falls into his hands.

'It's been such a mess David,' Morgan says gently. 'Such a mess. Once the truth was established, everyone told me that I should force you to listen, that you needed a good shaking down. But I felt that in telling you I would be seen as trying to exonerate myself, and I didn't want to do that. You have every reason to hate me, I'm not going to try and make out that I'm the innocent one in all of this. I'm just as guilty as McLaughlin.

'I just wanted you to know because the truth was worse than the truth you imagined and I wanted you to face it. For your own sake. At the same time I wanted you to make the choice to listen, I wanted *you* to come forward to ask *me*. But tonight I realised this wasn't ever likely to happen.

'It's all too much right now, but if I were you, David, I would take this truth and run with it, fly with it. We have, both of us, spent too long dwelling on something which is out of our control, which is finished. Not the memory of your mother, not the memories we have before I …. But the rest is finished. May is dead, McLaughlin is in prison. We can't change that. And we've got to stop trying.

'We have this farm. You have Nicola and your painting. There's so much left to build on. It would be foolhardy to throw it all away just because of what that man did. May wouldn't have wanted it. She never wanted to hurt either of us, no matter what she planned for herself. You have the rest of your life ahead of you David, and a lot of weight on your shoulders. How you deal with that weight now is up to you. But you're not answerable to either your mother or I. You are your own person, please don't let it mess you up, please don't.'

'My mother had an affair,' David suddenly snaps. He has raised his face and is glaring at his father. 'She lied to us. She lied to *me*. All that time she was planning to leave us. Then she was murdered by the same man she supposedly loved. In cold blood. My mother was *murdered*. Tell me, Dad. Just tell me. How can that not mess me up?'

David runs his finger along the chapped, dusty paint of the window sill then lifts it to the grimy pane. Slowly, meticulously, he carves a closed eye in the grime, its lashes long and heavy. A tear squeezes from the corner of the lid. He studies the drawing with an expression of deep concentration.

Pressing his palm against the glass, he violently scrubs it out before walking back to the chair and sitting down.

I sit up in the bed and watch him. It's barely dawn, the thin, blue light lurking around the edges of the curtain. He's naked and shivering.

He bows his head and studies the damp dust on his fingertips. A tear trickles down his chin and splatters lightly onto his bare knee. He turns his head away from me and studies the pictures of Sara.

'David?'

'I don't want to talk about it.'

He shakes his head numbly and sits with a vacant look. Even when the bursting, early morning sun scatters his pale body with golden light, he doesn't move, not even to brush away the tears which slide silently down his face.

That night, when he'd found out the truth about his mother's death, does not seem to have signalled the end of David's malady. In the days that follow, I begin to see the demons in his over-active mind stumbling to regroup, but instead of having a steady focus, their aim is confused. There's nowhere where he can dump his considerable fury, and now no single person to blame. And he knows that his mother, the one person whose memory had always soothed his fractured belief in human nature, had betrayed him too.

A different David is emerging, a David who I am afraid to approach. He's like a sleepwalker, a half-blind man, drugged and confused, who does not any longer know where he is and does not trust the hands reaching out to guide him.

He's stopped washing or caring how he looks. His hair is in a permanent tangle, his clothes splattered with cow dung and grass from the long, maddened walks he's begun taking around the farm, sometimes disappearing for hours on end. He tries to speak, to behave normally, but it's as if everything has become a struggle, as if day-to-day matters bewilder him. I find myself repeating questions and waiting in vain for answers.

Is it his mother's betrayal of him, or the violent nature of her death, which so disturbs him? I cannot help him if he will not speak about it, but it's as if after that night he has drawn the blinds on us all and is hiding in some dark, inaccessible place. He will not talk about his mother, will not talk about Kyle McLaughlin, and if I try to coax from him the excruciating pain I know he must be feeling, his reply is often incoherent.

'It's finished, finished, finished,' he cries one day after another futile probe. And when I reach out to hold his face in my hands, he clasps my forearms and holds them tightly to his cheeks. His tears dribble down my wrists.

His father, perhaps wiser than me, does not return to the subject in David's presence. But I can see in the older man's face the deep worry that his son's breakdown is causing.

For solace, David turns to drink once more, but even the whisky cannot bring relief. When I see him crash into bed each night, and wake the next morning with red eyes, it's clear that the alcohol is only exacerbating his pain.

I know that my responsibility is great. At night David clings to me like a drowning man clutching a raft. A strange neediness has emerged in him, a frenzied holding of my hands, a stroking of my hair whenever I'm in reach. Pulling me against him, he sits staring blindly ahead, pressing my face against his shoulder like a baby's as he rocks in his chair. Like a patient cat being cuddled by a child, I stay for him, though sometimes he holds me for hours.

Painting remains his only other comfort. Ironically, his agony is spurring the release of an unsurpassed brilliance in his work. Only on the phone to Caplan's do I hear the return of the old David. His tone is confident and articulate as he discusses the progress of his painting, the planning out of his display, the landscapes he's working on as well as a set of portraits he's painting of me. When not madly roaming the farm or clutching a bottle, he's sitting, trance-like, before his easel. It's his final retreat, the only time he can free his mind from the pain which has finally begun to unhinge him.

With the exhibition only two weeks away, he reaches inside and pulls out a final, frayed bravery, rising to the pressure with silent determination, the canvasses appearing like newspapers off a press. Still silent, still surly, he acts as if his survival depends on having no time to think about his mother and McLaughlin, and he begins rising early in the morning and working until late evening. From this point on he lives only for his painting and if he speaks, he speaks only of that.

Although I know that it's his way of coping, his absorption in his work becomes so great that I'm forced to remind him of our plans. His preoccupation with fixing up the shed and leaving the farmhouse, as with everything we had discussed, has now been buried under the slurry of the dreadful revelation. His only focus is the approach of the exhibition.

But it is I who am still sane and I find myself torn between sympathy and the need to move forward. I am becoming dissatisfied, more restless now than David to escape the confines of this crumbling farmhouse. It is my boredom with silent days either acting as a mute model, or left to my own devices, which is throwing the shadow of my past back over the vision of my future. Once more, my dreams have become tortured by unwanted images of a bloodstained floor and a face full of contempt.

And as each day passes and the river's voice grows louder, I am made aware yet again of its uncontrollable currents, its secret depths. As fear starts eating away at my newfound security, I become determined that I cannot, and will not, be left as another silent sacrifice to David's plight.

Chapter Nineteen

One morning, a week after the anniversary, I'm woken by David rising as the early dawn light steals into our attic room. Watching him dress from a pretence of sleep, I no longer bother to ask him where he's going.

He closes the door gently behind him. I close my eyes and picture him walking through the dawn mists.

After drowsing for several more hours, I finally rise from the warm bed. Getting dressed quickly, I pad down to the sunlit kitchen and look out of the window. I spot him in the distance, hunched over his easel by the barns, sketching the newborn calves as they stagger around after their mothers.

I glance down at the heavy steel watch which Morgan has left on the dresser. Audrey is bringing us a stock of old furniture which she's had rotting in her basement since her husband left her two years ago. She did not want anything left in her house which reminded her of him, so away it went, resulting in a very expensive refit which, she informs us, has been worth every penny.

I sluice off the crockery left from David's breakfast and am just placing the last dish on the draining board when I hear Morgan descending the stairs. He smiles when he sees me, but his face is filled with its usual strain.

'I was just about to wake you,' he says. 'Where's David? Did you tell him about the furniture?'

'Yes. He's painting near the barns. He's probably forgotten.'

'Should I go and tell him? He should really be helping.'

I sigh and shake my head.

'Let's leave him, John. I'm sure we'll cope.'

He begins to move silently around the kitchen, picking up letters and bills and putting them into a neat pile as I make him a cup of coffee. At last he sits down in the rocking chair. He reaches for the newspaper but does not open it. Blowing on the coffee, he watches me closely and says, 'This must be very difficult for you.'

'Sometimes.'

'But what can we do? How can we help him? I'm worried that there's more to this Nicola, I think he should be seeing a specialist. He's grown so emotionally unstable these last few years that I wonder if he's got a ....'

'I don't agree,' I interrupt. 'I just think he's in shock, that's all. It's hardly surprising. He'll get over it.'

Morgan turns to the window.

'I thought telling him the truth would straighten things out. But it's just made him worse. It's like he's – I don't know – gone so far into himself he can't find the way out.'

'At least he's still got his work.'

'But what about you? How long are you going to be able to tolerate this? He barely talks to you.'

I straighten and look out of the window over my soap-sudded hands.

'Has Audrey got a blue van?'

'James has.'

'This is him, then.'

'Right.' He rises wearily and comes to stand beside me.

We watch the vehicle bob its way up the uneven drive, the sunlight glinting on the windscreen. There's a slam of doors and James leaps from the driver's seat, his face glowing. Audrey gets out behind him.

They open the doors without knocking. Audrey comes in first, entering the kitchen with her usual flurry, plonking her handbag on the table and clasping her hands together. Her pale lips flash a smile in Morgan's direction.

160

'Lovely mornin' John. We've got it all here.'

'This is very kind of you Audrey.'

'It's nothin'. Been wantin' to get rid of it for ages.'

James follows with a cardboard box full of cushions. He smiles at Morgan. 'Hallo there, Doc. Where can I dump this?'

'David said to put everything in the drawing room,' I say.

'Did he now?' says Morgan, turning to me, 'I hope he's paying for storage.'

James stands there awkwardly until Morgan nods. 'Go through. You know where it is.'

James returns empty-handed, his fine hair falling across his face. Immediately I feel his gaze on me, his brow rising with a scarcely concealed look of disapproval.

'Heard you were still here. How's the love nest coming along?'

'Slowly.'

I struggle to keep the coldness from my tone but I'm aware of Morgan turning to look at me.

'Rightio.' James's tone is unnatural and stilted. 'Glad to be of service. Let's get this show on the road then, shall we?'

Audrey and I watch from the window as the two men crunch over the gravel towards the van and emerge a few minutes later with a heavy, dirty, cream sofa. They drag and bully it through the sunlight until they reach the kitchen door. It takes three attempts before the sofa is at the correct angle to get it past the door's large oak frame, then they push it through the kitchen. Morgan's face is red and he puffs heavily.

'Where's David?' James snaps as he comes out of the drawing room and brushes dust off his hands. 'He should bloody well be doing this.'

'He's painting.'

'Oh yeah, the exhibition. Mum told me.'

Morgan nods.

'Caplan's as well – they're big news.' He leans heavily against the Aga rail, his high chin and confident expression a shining model of England's privately educated middle class. His tone is patronising, as if he knows deep-down that he has nothing to envy David for, that his own position in life has already been secured.

''Course,' Audrey mutters, 'it would 'ave been better if he'd finished his education. Painting's a bit of a risky career if you ask me. But still ….'

'Don't be daft Mum!' James laughs. 'What does Dave need to go to Uni for? He's always been an artist – there's nothing anyone can teach him.'

Audrey smiles at Morgan.

'Well, it's the life, isn't it John? James 'as got so many friends.'

Her son winces and casts another look in my direction.

Morgan rises, his face impatient. 'Any more in there?'

'Yep,' James replies, his eyes still on my face. 'There's a couple of cupboards, a mattress, stuff like that.'

'Let's get on then, shall we?'

They bring the rest of the furniture in as I make tea. Audrey watches them, her hands on her hips, her lips pursed. I feel she has something on her mind. She's too silent for Audrey, too intent on watching the men when normally she would use an opportunity like this to fish for information.

After several minutes, I know she will feel forced to break the deadlock, to say anything rather than deal with the embarrassment of standing wordlessly in this sunlit kitchen. Audrey, I know, finds silence as oppressive as an unwanted embrace. Words are her way of freeing herself, of avoiding confrontation.

162

After a minute or so she begins to drum the sink lightly with her fingers. Then she says, 'The doctor doesn't seem 'imself these days.'

I nod.

'Still havin' trouble with David?'

'I guess.'

'That lad's goin' off the rails. The whisky he's buying ... I suppose he's learnt the truth at last?'

I pour the tea and do not answer.

'I mean, fancy putting his father through all that. I had the greatest respect for May of course, but really, the boy should've listened.'

Her gaze rests stubbornly on me. Finding only silence she turns and watches Morgan as he comes up the path to the front door, James striding behind him.

'That's it then. All done,' Morgan gasps.

'There's a couple of curtains on the front seat,' James says suddenly. 'I'll grab them before we go.'

''Course it's a bit dusty,' Audrey confesses. 'You'll have to give it a good scrub down.'

'Dirty isn't the word,' James laughs as he picks up his tea. 'I've seen cleaner stuff on a tip.'

His mother raises her eyebrows. 'I could say the same about your bedroom.' She winks at Morgan. 'I don't know – off they go to university – you'd expect them to come back a bit more domesticated. Not 'im. Dirty dustbin liner full of washing. Jeans to mend. Never stops, does it?'

'I wouldn't know Audrey,' Morgan says wearily.

'Course, no you wouldn't. I mean, your David doesn't mind the odd rip here and there does he? Still he's an artist I suppose.'

The allusion is obvious, David's unkempt appearance, his drinking, her sympathy for Morgan having to witness his son living the life of a vagabond and shaming all his former hopes for him.

'Oh put a sock in it Mum,' snaps James. 'He's just found out about his mother, what do you expect? Besides, David doesn't want to be like anyone else.'

Audrey Burrows throws her son a rueful glance and is silent.

'Anyway,' James continues, turning to me, 'talking about people not wanting to be anyone else – I remember now where I know you from. You remember me saying before – you looked familiar?'

I look at him blankly.

He takes a mouthful of tea then says casually, 'You're from Salisbury aren't you? You used to hang out at Mazim's Night Club.'

Morgan turns and stares at him. I shake my head, smile, and pick up a cloth to wipe some tea from the draining board.

'I doubt it,' I reply. 'Seeing as I've never been to Salisbury.'

He's silent but his face has a knowing expression. Though he has approached the subject casually, I realise that this is what all those looks have been about.

'Nicola is not very forthcoming about her past,' Morgan says archly. 'But she's quite adamant that she doesn't know Salisbury. It's one of the few insignificant pieces of information that I did manage to glean – which I always found strange considering the only road into Morton is the Salisbury road.'

Audrey nods and turns to me, but her look is disbelieving.

'I told 'im you weren't from there.'

'Strange,' James says, 'I mean, when I saw you in the Swan that day, I couldn't think where I'd seen you. When it came to me, I was sure it was you. I remember because, well, don't take offence, it's just that the lads and I used to think you were a bit of a corker.'

'*She* was, you mean.' I stare back at him. 'Thanks for the compliment but you're talking about someone else.'

There's an awkward pause. Audrey's eyes are glued to me and I know, suddenly, that a long discussion has preceded this moment.

But I'm not interested in what Audrey or her son think; it's Morgan's frozen expression which fills me with apprehension. He raises his head now, his unshaven chin pointing in my direction.

'So what happened to this Nicola look-alike?' he asks.

'Oh, God knows. It was a long time back and I went off to university. I mean, I never knew her to talk to – just used to see her in the bar. I do remember someone saying her old man was a bit of a shithead – I mean, "look but don't touch" kind of thing.'

'Funny that, isn't it?' Audrey says. 'Only the other day a woman swore she'd seen me in Newton Abbot. Newton Abbot I said? Never been there in me life. She was rock sure though.'

'Yes, incredible,' retorts Morgan.

'Well thank you very much for bringing it all over,' I say lightly, my hand gesturing toward the drawing room.

'No trouble.' James stands and hands me his mug.

'Thanks.'

Audrey fumbles with her handbag. 'Best be off then John. I'll be up for the eggs tomorrow.'

'I'd better get those curtains,' Morgan says.

I expect James to follow but he hangs on for a second and I feel his stare once again, penetrating and this time without humour. I turn and watch Audrey and Morgan chatting on the driveway. Suddenly, I feel his hand on my arm. He pulls me violently against him with an expression of cold determination. His mouth is almost on mine.

'David's my friend you know.'

165

I look into his eyes and feel my heart begin to pound.

'Let go of my arm.'

'I'm telling you …. I've been asking around about you and things don't seem to be adding up. I've not told Mum yet because I don't see the point in upsetting this family again for nothing. But believe me, I'm going to be making some enquiries, and if these rumours I'm hearing turn out to be true then you've got some serious questions to answer young lady.'

I feel his breath rasp against my face.

'Where is he Nicola?'

'You what?'

'I said, "Where is *he?*"'

I feel minute flecks of his spit hit my cheek. At that moment, Morgan enters the kitchen with a pair of gaudy, floral-patterned curtains in his arms. He comes to an abrupt halt, his eyes widening. James nods, face reddening, and leaves the kitchen in a hurry, before Morgan can ask any questions.

We watch in silence as the van bounces its way back down the drive. I imagine the conversation taking place over its wheel, James's heated insistence, his mother nodding in agreement.

'I think you've got some explaining to do, Nicola.'

Morgan has turned to face me, his face cold, his mouth buckling into a grimace. 'What was that all about?'

I push the hair from my face and shrug.

'Nothing. It's bullshit.'

Morgan moves to the window and looks out at the farm. His eyes, grave and uncertain in the sunlight, search the drive for the his son. 'Why did you say you'd never been to Salisbury?'

'Because I haven't – he's got me mixed up with someone else.' I move to the Aga and look down at the logs which Morgan has stacked ready for tonight's fire. My fingers find the splintered wood, brittle and ragged under my soft skin.

'I don't know, Nicola, it seems a bit odd to me. What was James saying to you just then? Something he didn't want me to hear, obviously.' He turns from the window, secure in the knowledge that David is not around, and looks at me intently, then gestures towards a chair. I don't move, my eyes meeting his in a cold challenge. We face each other for some moments without speaking. From the garden comes the cry of the cockerel.

I shrug. 'I don't understand you, John – why are you so eager to believe James and not me?'

'I've known James a long time.'

'Well, so what? Even if I have got a doppelganger in Salisbury, what's so important about it?'

'James seemed pretty sure it was you.'

'James lives up his own arse.'

'It'll come out in time you know.'

'What will?'

'Whatever it is you're hiding.'

The statement hangs in the room. As he stares at me, the sun's rays glance through the window and illuminate the slow whirl of his cigarette smoke. Outside, the cockerel crows once more and the noon chimes from Morton church sound from the hillside.

'I'm not hiding anything, John. I'm really not.'

He takes a deep breath. 'Nicola, I don't want my son to be hurt again. This is the final straw for him, learning about May. One more thing and that will be it.'

'I've no intention of hurting David.'

He flicks his ash into a saucer. 'I really hope not.'

'And what's that supposed to mean?'

'Just what it says. What about this ex of yours – from what James was saying he sounds like the jealous type. How do you know he's not looking for you? You tried to kill yourself because of him Nicola. What would you do if he showed up here, would you take him back?'

'You think I don't love David? You think that he's some rebound whim?'

'I didn't say that.'

'Then what *are* you saying?'

He rises slowly from the table.

'Because if that's a possibility – your ex appearing here – I'd rather you left now before David has to suffer yet another betrayal.'

His eyes find mine and I see that the threat is very real.

I turn away and sigh.

'He won't show up. I promise.'

'What makes you so sure?'

'For God's sake John, why can't you believe me? He isn't going to come here. And just look at the lives it would destroy if I left. Not just me and David. Not just you – but your grandchild's as well.'

'Then we'll just have to ….' He stops abruptly, his eyebrows rising as my words sink in.

'My *what?*'

'Your grandchild.'

He takes a step back, then another.

'You're pregnant?'

'Yes.'

He leans heavily against the dresser, his eyes dark with a mixture of emotion. He does not look at me but at the ground and I hear his breathing, ragged and heavy.

'Does David know?'

'Not yet. I'm going to tell him this evening. He knows something's up though.'

'And you'll …?'

168

'We'll keep it. This could be the thing to save him, to help him see that there's a future beyond this mess. He often talks about wanting kids.'

'You're sure you're really …?'

'I've still got the test.'

Morgan drops into a chair and looks at the backs of his hands. Outside the cows are lowing. It must be milking time.

'This is too much,' he says quietly.

I turn to the window and see David's distant figure moving against the backdrop of the cowsheds. His easel has gone and he's bending down, putting his sketches in a file. Behind him, Art and the cows trail slowly into the barn.

'I don't understand why you're so upset,' I say finally. 'Why have you got this crazy idea that I'm out to damage your son? He saved my life and gave me a reason to want to carry on living. Why would I want to hurt him?'

Morgan doesn't answer. I glance at him for a second then turn back to the window. David has begun making his way up the drive. He is stooped over his canvasses and easel but his head is raised and I know he's watching the outline of my figure behind the window.

I smile because, strangely, I can feel him smiling at me. Then I look up at the sky, which heralds promise of a beautiful day. It is cloudless and blue, and filled with swifts.

Chapter Twenty

And so the waiting game was over at last, putting down your key you smiled at me and you asked – 'Still one eye on the door, Nicola?'

Wordless, wrung out, I just stared and I fought with the question mark in my eye.

Too gentle for you, your wet lips on my brow. You pressed my shoulders, lifted my chin.

'Nicola, I got the message,' you said. 'But I'm out of here, it's time to say goodbye.'

You moved forwards, your hand stroking my cheek and I said – 'Just like that? What about the rent? What about the rest?'

Stepping back, I knew you'd decided to oil the screw. Too much, too kind, all of it, as kind as your first trip into my head when you pulled me into the trap door of your soul and you said, 'I'm going to take him away from you, Nicola.'

But now, with a still smile and an ironic look in your eye.

'Nicola, what do you want, my life?'

'Tell me,' I said. 'You owe me that at least.'

And so you told me, your soft voice sucking me against your chest, your hand reaching under my neck, muttering your smug condolences. And I did not fight, my body slumped as I heard your words, drawing the curtain on our life, my hand reaching behind me in the sink, searching coldly, numbly, for the knife.

Chapter Twenty One

Bristol is freezing. A hard wind gallops up from the river and rips at our hair as we get out of the car. I pull my coat around me and shiver next to David, who seems far away, his eyes moving over the docks. Below our feet the water lashes the numerous fishing boats which clutter the harbour. The sky is a panic of screaming gulls. Behind us, the traffic in the evening rush hour screeches its way along the water's edge.

I take David's hand and squeeze it tightly as I survey the numerous old buildings which overlook the estuary. It feels bizarre to be in a city after so many weeks at Morgan's farm. The rush of people to my left and right is something I've long forgotten after so many steady, unchanging days. I stare with fascination at the random assortment of characters who pass: a gaggle of old ladies totter by, their gloved hands clutching Marks and Spencer bags, a woman wearing a cashmere shawl and holding a large, scarlet umbrella steps gracefully along the pavement in high heels. And teenagers in school uniform, waiting at bus stops and sharing their last cigarette from a packet of ten – or simply sitting on walls and watching the world go by.

The sky is a bitter grey behind the boat masts. I shiver once more as the wind picks up my collar and sends it slamming against the back of my neck. I clutch David's arm tightly.

'Where is this place?' demands Morgan as he locks the car door.

David turns reluctantly from the water's edge and points across the busy road to a small, cobbled alley which winds its way between two boutiques.

'Up there, behind those shops.'

Beyond the belching traffic I see old-fashioned signs hanging on fine iron chains advertising a variety of cafes and gift shops.

Their lights beam warmly behind misted windows. My gaze follows the cobbled lane past the shops to a large sign at the far end of the alley. In green and gold writing I made out the swirling letters: 'Caplan's'.

'It's pretty posh,' David says blankly.

He struggles to light a cigarette as the bitter wind tears the flame from his Zippo. He's shaking, both with cold and fear, and he swears quietly to himself as he struggles with the lighter. Sensing his nervousness, I step before him and cup my hands to block the draft.

'Don't worry – they're not going to eat you.'

He shakes his head. Behind him Morgan fidgets. 'C'mon David, we're late already.'

David takes several long, nervous drags, inhaling deeply and holding the smoke deep in his lungs. Then he throws the half-smoked cigarette into the gutter. Watching him, I feel pleased for the timing of this exhibition. It has distracted him from pain which has become so deeply ingrained I sometimes fear he will never recover.

Knowledge of my pregnancy is the only other thing which brightens his face and mention of it always brings excitement to his voice. From the firm way he takes my arm at this moment, I sense his awareness of it. Suddenly I feel certain that his realisation of this undeniable future must surely necessitate his eventual recovery.

'There won't be many people there,' he murmurs. 'Just dealers and critics – maybe some friends of Caplan.'

Morgan nods and strides forward. David's hand, tight on my wrist, guides me with exaggerated care around slow-moving bonnets.

We walk up to the large panel of glass which marks the front of Caplan's. My attention is drawn to the familiar reproduction of the hawk which they have used to advertise the exhibition. The posters are larger than the original, each one is framed and hangs from a pale green partition which blocks the inside of the shop from sight. All the paintings carry the same picture, the hawk in full flight. The copy reads: 'Released and Other Paintings', by David Morgan.

'Released?' I murmur, looking at David curiously.

'They chose it – they didn't give me much say.'

I look at the posters. They're framed in the same green and gold as Caplan's sign. Sara's wings are outstretched against a clear blue sky, her talons diving for a kill as her dark eyes flash out of the painting.

'I wanted them to use one of you,' David explains. 'But their customers seem to like the hawk most.' He looks at the poster and I realise, noticing the shadow which passes over him, that he's remembering his bird.

'Seems like a long time ago now,' I say softly.

He sighs and turns away. 'Come on,' he says. 'Let's go inside, I'm cold.'

Morgan is waiting for us in the doorway. 'Are we all ready then?'

David shrugs, moving toward his father with reluctant steps. Morgan pats his shoulder. 'Come on, son, it's your moment.'

David enters the large foyer and stares wide-eyed at the various listings posters which cover the tall, polished oak walls. Though the room is not large, our footsteps echo as we walk carefully up the three oak steps and into the reception area. Two men in bow ties and an elegantly dressed woman stand in front of the desk, conversing loudly. David pauses, watching them warily, then lifts his head and swings round to inspect the high, arching ceiling with its modern, diamond-shaped starlight and bright murals.

Morgan and I wait. I glance toward him and see he is watching his son. But I sense by the uncomfortable way he turns that he can feel my gaze on him. I step forward and take David's arm. We approach the reception desk together.

A prim-looking woman with bobbed red hair frowns up from a list of names.

'Have you been invited? This is a private exhibition. We're open to the public tomorrow.'

'I'm the artist,' David replies quietly. 'This is my father, John Morgan, and my girlfriend.'

She looks flustered. Flicking casually through her papers, she smiles sweetly and ticks her list. 'Terribly sorry. Can I take your invitations please?'

She looks up at me curiously as I hand mine over. 'Well of course. You're the girl from the paintings.'

'Not so beautiful in real life,' I reply, smiling.

'Or simplistic,' Morgan chips in.

David darts a curious look at his father. The latter smiles back at him grimly.

We make our way downstairs to the large oak-panelled doors at the back of the foyer, where two more reproductions of the hawk are hung. David looks pale as he takes off his long coat and reveals the expensive, dark-brown suit he has borrowed from his father. He pulls at his tie awkwardly. Morgan also wears a suit and I am in a long, low-cut black dress of May Morgan's.

Morgan turns to his son. 'Ready then?'

Morgan pushes open the doors to reveal a long, softly lit, underground corridor. The paintings have been displayed along both sides, each one under its own, individual light.

We are greeted by a murmur of animated discussion. Seven or eight people mill around the corridor, all elegantly dressed in expensive-looking smart suits and long, graceful dresses. They stand in front of the pictures holding wine glasses and speaking to each other in hushed voices. Several of them turn as David enters the room. A tall man with an aquiline face throws him a curious glance and turns and whispers to his partner, a thin woman in a velvet dress. I sense David's awkwardness, his feeling of things being over his head as he pauses and takes my hand in a tight grip.

There is a loud exclamation from our right.

'David, there you are!'

A huge man is upon us, his face flushed salmon-pink and his thick grey hair cropped short to disguise its rapid balding. He wears a black suit which is still stretched tight across his enormous girth as he looms above us and roars, 'Glad you all made it. Got a bit worried there for a moment.'

'This is George Caplan,' David says. 'This is my father, Dr John Morgan, and my girlfriend, Nicola.'

He shakes our hands vigorously and slaps David hard across the shoulders.

The tall man with the aquiline face has turned to stare at us.

'It's not looking bad David, not bad at all. We've got the *Bristol Post* here and the *Western Gazette*, they're pretty gobsmacked. Tried to get *The Guardian*, no luck – but if the *Post* give it a clean bill of health we'll soon have 'em sniffing. Got wine? No? Can't have that. Lucy, where in God's name are you?'

I like Caplan. He's warm and jovial, and I notice with some amusement the conspiring edge in his voice, as if he believes that life is one great joke and wants to share it with us. In his presence, I see the light returning to David's eyes, the old youthful excitement, for Caplan has that energy which makes all life's problems seem suddenly surmountable, even welcome. Everything is about challenge, he seems to be saying, everything is about learning to laugh at the unlaughable.

He whirls around and I step back to avoid his impressive stomach. He rolls his eyes, but I'm not sure whether it's from frustration with the missing Lucy or ridicule of his immaculate-looking guests.

'Stupid cow's probably drunk it all herself. S'cuse me a sec.'

We watch him storm down the corridor in search of wine, tapping people on the shoulder as he passes. David grins.

'A character,' Morgan remarks as he watches his son with cautious pleasure. 'Doesn't seem like the arty type though.'

David nods. 'Oh, he knows what a load of old pomp it all is. When this has finished he'll be down the Black Goose knocking back double gins with the locals. He doesn't give a shit about these tossers ....'

It's almost as if he checks himself on purpose, this sudden gabbling excitement. His face flushes and he looks down.

'So why does he do it?' Morgan asks carefully, eager to preserve his son's mood.

'Money of course – he's stinking rich.'

David turns away from us, his face clouding. He walks slowly past the elegantly attired critics, some of whom are now more interested in studying him than the paintings. David has already told me about Caplan's rate of success with these exhibitions – Stephen Heath, Caplan's last discovery, now fields shows in Paris and Brussels – these people know that David is someone to watch.

Wandering through the corridor and studying the paintings that I already know so well, I think how I have always liked his work – but seeing it here now, beautifully framed and hung side by side, I know exactly why Caplan has chosen David as an artist worth exhibiting. The colour springs from every painting, the bleak and the bright placed in juxtaposition, winter and summer alternatively. There is the hawk in the bitter autumn wind, with a backdrop of greys and browns, and the young calves, stumbling after their mothers in the bright spring sunshine. His use of the brush brings the world alive. The skies whirl and the wind blusters, the grass hums with insects or squelches with mud, even the flowers seem to sway in an early summer breeze.

Caplan returns with a tray of flutes, a huge grin on his face.

'Going well David. You've knocked their socks off. Thought you might.'

David's face flushes with pleasure.

'But of course,' Caplan exclaims, gawping at me. 'You're the model. We've got you in the other room – down at the back. Why don't you and Dad here go have a look while Dave and I have a quick chat?'

Morgan, who has declined the wine, follows me reluctantly to the door at the furthest end of the corridor.

We enter a smaller, darker room and here I am, hanging on all four walls in all my various postures, each picture individually lit by a small lamp. Because David has always painted me in soft light, the contrast of silver and shadow on my skin in the darkness of the exhibition room is striking, as if I'm really there, staring out of the night like some kind of ethereal creature.

'Of course, if he gets famous you'll have to stop modelling for him,' remarks Morgan.

'Why's that?'

'Wouldn't like your ex to see you staring out of some painting, would you?'

I don't answer because I know there's no point. We remain in the small room without speaking, our eyes on the paintings but our thoughts on each other.

Morgan has been like this ever since the morning that Audrey and James brought the furniture. Though he's not openly aggressive, he has changed toward me. I see it in his sideways looks. Then there are the underhand comments, the insistence that I should come clean about whatever it is I'm hiding. I'm not sure which bothers him most, James' insistence that he has seen me before, or my pregnancy.

With a sudden feeling of tiredness, I turn away and walk towards the door. 'I'm going back,' I say quietly. 'I want to know what Caplan's been saying.'

Morgan turns and nods. I hear his footsteps following me as I make my way past the group of wine-drinking critics. David is by the entrance. He's standing alone, his face turned to the wall.

'They're taking it to London,' he whispers. 'They've already sold four paintings.'

He turns and his large eyes meet mine. His face is pale underneath his dark curls and he doesn't smile. In fact he looks completely numb, as if somebody has just told him some awful piece of news.

Morgan smiles at his son over his glasses. 'I think this calls for a celebration. We'll get some champagne on our way home.'

David nods. 'Let's get Art up.'

'Art was fishing today, it's his day off.'

Caplan marches over and interrupts us. 'Sure you've heard the news. Bet you're proud as punch.'

Morgan nods, looking like a pea next to a drum as the huge man smacks him around the shoulders.

'I always thought he had talent,' he says.

'Talent?' barks Caplan. 'You've no idea what's going to happen after we get to London. They'll swoop in for the kill – a landscapist like David doesn't come along very often. Listen David, I think it's about time you met some of these horrors.'

I watch as the enormous man leads David over to meet the various guests. The skinny man with the aquiline face edges towards them and shakes his hand with a simpering expression, then beckons to his partner. David clutches his glass of wine and nods vigorously as he answers their questions with an incredulous face. His meek, somewhat abashed manner is that of a tramp who has just entered a palace. It doesn't seem possible that all this is for him, the scruffy young man who lives in a damp shed and drinks cheap whisky.

Driving back to Morton we cannot shut him up. He leans between the head rests and chatters on and on about the remarks people made and the forthcoming exhibition in London. I watch the profile of his face in the car's darkness and think how like a child he sounds, his fingers gripping the chair's edge as his excited eyes constantly turn from his father to me. He's relieved and astounded by his own success, proud, unable to stop talking as if talking makes it real and silence will turn it back into some distant dream. The memory of his mother and McLaughlin is all but forgotten.

'We'll be able to build a cottage, Nicola – where the shed is. I know we can't live in that place now, not with the baby, but we can afford to build something there instead. Caplan thinks all the paintings will be sold in London.'

'Don't count your chickens David,' his father says sternly, his eyes on the road. But I can hear the pleasure in his voice. It's a long time since he has seen his son so happy.

'I know. But remember Steven Heath – he was the artist Caplan promoted last year – he's raking it in now, the dealers are queuing up for his stuff. Caplan said I knock spots off him.'

His father smiles as he pulls off the motorway.

'Can't you step on it Dad? I want to catch Art at the pub.'

'I've only just got my licence back David, I'm not about to lose it for Art's sake.'

'I'll have to get another hawk, a Sara II.' David rambles on. 'They loved the paintings of her.'

179

'It wouldn't have the same feeling behind it,' Morgan says quietly. 'It would be like using another model instead of Nicola.'

He shoots me a look over his shoulder. I stare back at him coldly.

'No, I couldn't do that ....' David shudders. 'I suppose you're right. It's all about feeling, not the object but the feeling you have for it. I guess there's enough animals on the farm to keep me going.'

Morgan draws into Morton and pulls the car up outside Burrow's stores. Though it's dark I notice that the river, under the village's bright street lamp, has almost dried up from the early spring heat. There is just a slow trickle now, meandering its way through the village green.

'What's the time?' Morgan asks.

David glances at his watch. 'Six thirty.'

'Let's go for a drink – you still want to see Art, don't you?'

'At the Swan?'

'Where else?'

David stares at the back of his father's head with amazement.

'But you haven't been in there since ... I mean, I can just nip in and tell him, there's no need for you to ....'

'There's a time for everything, David. Come on, let's celebrate. I want to get some bubbly anyway. Not for me mind and you'd better not have too much Nicola.'

David looks at me as Morgan gets out of the car. He shakes his head. 'I can't believe it. God the old man's got some nerve – he hasn't been in there since Mum died. They're gonna have him for breakfast.'

He shrugs, his eyes on mine. Running a finger through my hair, he leans over the seat quickly and kisses my cheek. Then he opens the door and strides after Morgan.

I can see that Morgan is being brave in stepping back into his old drinking haunt. But I also know that this is all for David, the son who has returned to the nest. I know that Morgan cannot get enough of this new, rambling, happy David, the shadows swept aside, all temporarily forgotten in the wake of his sudden, overwhelming success.

I watch them through the window as they stand and chat and find myself examining their new rapport with a careful eye. They're waiting for me, their hands in their pockets, the wind in their hair, and Morgan's face is turned toward the pub, uncertain.

David walks back to the car and knocks on the window. His face has a questioning look.

Fumbling for the handle, I recognise a certain irony about the situation. How ordinary Morgan and David look now, just a father and son going for a pint and a chat. No one would believe that only recently Morgan was lying on the kitchen floor, his face covered in blood from David's fist.

'Ready then Dad?' David says briskly as his father pauses in the doorway, his gaunt face suddenly pale with uncertainty under the pub's bright sign.

David glances at me as he speaks, his eyes narrowing as if he can't believe what his father is about to do. An awkward silence follows. Morgan shrugs, his casual gesture betrayed by a look of nervous anticipation.

He pushes open the door and the warmth of the pub is upon us. There's a garble of Wiltshire accents and the smell of log smoke from the large, open fire. Nobody notices us at first, they're locked away in their conversations. There's a hush, then faces turn one by one, their eyes looking us up and down, taking in our smart clothes, our travel-weary faces. About five or six men stand at the bar staring at the peculiar sight, not only of Morgan but Morgan with his son, the son they all know hates his guts. I see Morgan pause, his eyes moving cautiously over the men's faces as he looks for Art, who is not here. He walks to the bar. The colour rises in his cheeks.

Nobody speaks as we move up to join him. A few of the men nod to David then turn their eyes back to Morgan.

'Evening' John.' Paddy, Art's friend, sits at his usual table. He lifts a stiff hand in greeting then drops it. Morgan nods in reply, eyes flickering with surprise.

Grace comes out of the kitchen and places some bottles on a shelf. She turns curiously, aware of the silence, surveying her customers until her gaze reaches Morgan. He smiles at her grimly, his fingers playing nervously with a twenty-pound note.

'John, what a surprise!'

'Good evening Grace, it's been a long time hasn't it? I'll have a mineral water please, and whatever these two want.'

The woman looks at him and nods, as if waking from a trance.

'Evenin' John.' Morgan turns to see a small, grey-haired man signalling to him across the bar. He raises his hand in return.

'Good evening, Jack.'

'Let me get these for you. Good to see you proppin' up the bar again.'

'Instead of it propping me up. Thank you Jack, that's very kind.'

'No trouble. An' I'll 'ave a Bass Grace.'

The little man pulls out a ten-pound note. He rubs his nose self-consciously with an old handkerchief. People in the pub begin to chat quietly again.

Morgan's face creases into a smile. His look of nervousness passes slowly into pleasure and slight astonishment.

'Of course he used to be popular,' David says, leading me to a table. 'He's a generous man, as you've noticed. Used to buy a lot of rounds. I mean, they criticised him a lot after the accident, but it was really because he stopped coming down here. Drinkers don't like to see a fellow member leave the roost.'

We sit down in a corner and watch Morgan in animated conversation with several men.

'It's almost like you were never enemies now,' I say.

David takes a sip of his drink and reaches for my hand under the table. His fingers examine mine. Then he sighs. 'You've been so patient with me Nicola, these last few weeks. I'll never forget that. I know what a pathetic, infantile arsehole I've been, and I can't pretend that tomorrow I won't be the same again. It's taking time for what Art told me to sink in. You live with this idea in your head and everything you do surrounds it. Then someone comes along and turns the whole lot upside down.'

He breaks off for a second, a shadow falling across his face. He squeezes my hand. 'But tonight I want to forget about hating my father. I can't forget it was him who allowed you to stay and without you none of this would have been possible. You've given me back everything I've lost.'

He shrugs, his face falling. Then the words come out in a long release of tightly held breath. 'It's just that I've never loved anything or anyone as much as this in my whole life. It's as if it's in my chest every time I look at you. It hurts. Do you know that? How can something which makes us feel good actually cause us physical pain? When I paint you, I'm aware of the most delicate things about you. I can suddenly notice, for instance, how beautiful your left eyebrow is. Yet when I try to conjure up your face, I can't even remember what you look like. It's all floating and muddled.'

He's gripping my hand but his head is turned away.

I pick up my glass and drink the last of my beer.

'It's good,' he says under his breath, so quietly that I can barely hear him. 'It's so good.'

Morgan appears over his shoulder carrying two more drinks for us. He sits down and grins broadly.

'I can't believe it,' he says.

Morgan's voice is no longer weary, but high with excitement. He sounds like a young man. His eyes shine and for once the frown has left his face, leaving him looking years younger. It's difficult, most of the time, to see Morgan as handsome, yet with his dark grey suit and recently-cut hair, he has suddenly repossessed a youthful animation.

David gulps down the remains of his beer and reaches for the fresh one. 'How do you feel about being a grandfather Dad? What with all that's happened, the way I've been ....' He stops for a second. '... Well, we haven't really been able to talk about it, have we?'

Morgan's smile flickers. He nods his head at his son but the light in his face has faded at the unwelcome reminder. David stiffens.

'Is it a problem?'

Morgan shakes himself and forces a smile. 'No, no not at all. It was a bit of a shock when Nicola told me, that's all.' He pauses, drawing on his cigarette. 'Maybe I'm just old fashioned – but it all seems a little fast.' His brow furrows as he sets down his mineral water and looks at it thoughtfully. 'Couldn't drink too much of this,' he murmurs.

'The low alcohol beers are pretty good nowadays,' David says, moving his chair to stand up. 'I'll get you one.'

Morgan shakes his head and puts a hand on his son's arm.

'No, even the taste of it might set me off. It's better to leave well alone.' He rises from the table. 'I'll get the bubbly.'

He goes to the bar and is immediately surrounded by the men again. There's more laughter and the smile returns to Morgan's face. Even the sullen Paddy has risen to join them.

I turn back to David. 'He's not very happy about it, is he?'

David's face is troubled. He takes a long drink from his pint and looks at his father. Then he lights a cigarette and inhales deeply. 'Who cares what he thinks anyway? Fuck him. Just because we're talking again, it doesn't mean he's going to take over my life.'

'I don't know David,' I say quietly, 'I feel in some ways – I mean – well perhaps we should leave Morton.'

He turns to me with a questioning look.

'We can still live in the countryside,' I continue. 'You know, in a cottage somewhere quiet, somewhere you can paint. It's just, I don't know. I'd like to get away from here. There's too much gossip – and your dad, he's not so keen now that I'm a permanent fixture.'

David exhales a large smoke ring and takes the last mouthful of his drink. 'You're really sure that's what you want?' he says, his gaze travelling around the bottom of his glass.

'Yes. Yes I think so.'

He shrugs. 'Makes no difference to me. In fact it might do me good to paint new landscapes. Maybe we could go to Scotland, somewhere like that. There's plenty of wild birds up there. Ospreys. I could get into Ospreys ….'

I say nothing but grip his hand tightly. He looks at me uncertainly, then smiles broadly and leans over to kiss me.

We wait as Morgan rounds off his conversation with the men. There are a lot of slaps on backs. He returns to the table and looks down at us. 'Ready then?'

'What about Art?' David asks.

Morgan shakes his head. 'Paddy says he's not at home. Hasn't come back from his fishing.'

David shrugs and rises from the table. 'Never mind, it'll have to be a family-only affair.'

As we drive back to the farm, all our moods are bright. David is quite drunk and he begins singing to himself quietly. Morgan seems elated – he smiles widely, his thoughts probably still on his warm reception at the pub and the rapid and welcome change in his son. The chilled bottle of champagne sits in David's lap.

It is the blackest of nights. The moon and stars are obscured by a thick blanket of fast-moving cloud. Morgan drives steadily, his eyes fixed on the road as the car's headlights pick out snakes of tree limbs and branches before swinging onwards. The first splatter of rain hits the windscreen. I watch as Morgan turns on the wipers and lifts an unlit cigarette to his mouth. We pass the stile and make our way slowly towards the farm.

'Hello, that's strange.'

David lifts his head. 'What?'

'The kitchen lights are on.'

I look between the two head rests. Morgan's right, the windows beckon their warmth as we draw up to the house.

'Art's here,' I say. 'There's his van, over by the gate.'

Morgan relaxes. With a sigh of relief he opens the car door and steps on to the gravel.

'Wonder what he wants. Doesn't usually come in if I'm not around.' He moves toward the house. 'Come on, let's get inside.'

David takes my hand and follows his father, who waits for him in the porch.

Another splatter of rain coats our shoulders. Morgan pulls the latch down and opens the kitchen door. But he does not enter. Instead he simply stands, his thin body barring our way. I see his frail shoulders stiffen.

David shifts impatiently. 'C'mon, Dad, what's the hold-up?'

Morgan doesn't move. I rise onto tiptoes and crane my neck over his shoulder. I can see Art sitting in the rocking chair. He's looking at Morgan with an empty expression.

'C'mon.' David gives his father a gentle push. 'Art mate, c'mon it's time to celebrate.' He lifts the bottle of champagne in the air. 'I'm gonna be fam ....'

He stops short, and his body goes still. He's looking where Morgan is looking. I follow his gaze.

On the old oak table is a large, grey blanket, its edges unfolded to reveal its contents. The smell and sight hits me at the same time as it hits David. Lying on the blanket, putrefied and decomposed, is the body of a dead baby.

Chapter Twenty Two

From the hillside comes the sound of Morton's church bells announcing the evening service, the solemn chimes carried towards us on the gathering wind, a wind which builds in strength as it hurries in from the open land surrounding the north side of the farm. Its footsteps circle the house.

I stare at the tiny corpse.

Behind me I hear a gagging noise. I turn briefly and see David through the open door. He's bent over on the drive, his hands clutching his stomach as its contents spray out over the gravel.

Art has turned the main light on. It's a modern striplight, completely unsuitable for such an old fashioned kitchen. I understand now why Morgan rarely uses it, always preferring the small lamp he keeps on the dresser. This light has no sympathy, it's garish, wiping out all subtle shades and shadows. It glares down now on this thing that looks more like an old man than a child, and cruelly highlights the deep purple swelling of it neck, the rank river weed which dribbles from its open mouth. The face is chalk white, the eyes open, the pupils sunk back into their sockets as if a pair of thumbs has forced them there.

Morgan and Art stare at each other in silence. Morgan approaches the table and looks down at the child over his gold-rimmed glasses. His voice, thin and sickened, sounds as if it comes from far off. 'Where did you find it?'

'In the river.'

'You were fishing?'

Art nods. 'Water's down. Saw it in the mud.'

I look up to see open disgust on Morgan's face. His skin is almost as white as the corpse's, and I wonder if he's also fighting the need to vomit.

He stares at the child in silence. Almost as a reflex action, he lights a cigarette and turns his face toward the kitchen window. He inhales deeply and lets the smoke go in a long release. Behind me, I hear David return to the kitchen. I glance at his pale, stricken face, the vomit on the collar of his chocolate-coloured suit. He still holds the bottle of champagne.

Morgan looks at his son then down at the corpse. 'It looks as if it could only have been a few weeks old. What's that around its neck?'

Art sits back in the rocking chair. 'Shoelace,' he says, turning his gaze towards me.

'What happened to it?' David says. 'Was it drowned?'

Morgan touches the child's neck gently. 'It's too early to say yet,' he says quietly. 'But I would say it's been strangled. It must have been weighted so it wouldn't be discovered.' He fingers the rotten pockets of a tiny, tattered green jacket.

Art nods, meeting his gaze. 'Aye, there were. Couple of rocks in the lining. I took 'em out.'

David steps forward and places the bottle of champagne onto the dresser. His fingers find my arm. 'What kind of sick bastard …?' He shudders. 'Where'd you find it Art?'

'In the Dale, under the bridge,' Art replies flatly.

I do not look at David or Morgan. Instead I look at the corpse, its body caked in dry mud. I observe the cracked lips, the skin on the forehead which has been diced from the constant movement of flint and pebble, the thin blonde locks, matted like dead horse hair, woven with stone and weed. The little mouth seems frozen in a final scream.

Morgan shakes himself. Lifting the cigarette to his mouth with an unsteady hand, he walks slowly to the window. He stares out into the darkness.

'Well, you've really done it now.'

David looks at his father, his expression perplexed. It's not clear who Morgan is talking to, if indeed he is talking to anyone at all.

'What shall we do?' the younger man says finally. 'Hadn't we better call the police?'

The church bells have finished, the only sound now is the wind which pounds the house with growing energy. Morgan turns but doesn't answer him. Instead he looks at me.

'Well what do you think Nicola?' What do *you* think we should do?'

I cup a palm and stare at it.

'It's a brown shoelace, isn't it Art?' he asks.

'Aye.'

'Made of leather, the same?'

'Looks the same.'

David stares at his father. 'What are you talking about? The same as what?'

There is silence. I glance up to see Morgan's face dissolve. His lips press together and his thin mouth begins to quiver. He throws back his head and looks at the ceiling. David takes a step forward, his fingers dropping from my arm. He looks at his father with confusion as the latter's face collapses into a kind of agony, then turns to Art, who rocks back and forward in the chair and won't meet David's eye.

'What are you suggesting?' There is a sudden coldness in David's voice.

For a few seconds no one answers. It's as if neither Art nor Morgan can bring themselves to reveal the truth. David's gaze swings from Art back to his father.

'What the fuck is going on?'

'It's 'er shoelace,' Art replies finally. 'She was missing' one when you found her. I gave 'er another one.'

190

David turns to him with a face caught between shock and disbelief. Several seconds pass. He takes a step towards me and smiles. 'Oh *come on*, it could be anyone's shoelace.'

I watch two strong creases form in his cheeks, as if he's listening to a good story. He's immobile, suspended, his eyes wide and shining as he waits for someone to break the silence, to announce the worst of jokes. No one smiles back. He looks into Art's blank, empty face and at the same time a voice in his head must be whispering that nobody is that sick, that low-minded to make a joke out of something like this.

He turns back to the child and the smile leaves his face.

'That's ridiculous.'

'It's true.' My words are barely audible but I see the muscles on the back of David's neck stiffen.

He turns to face me and in his face I see the same irony, on his mouth, the same incredulous smile.

'Don't be stupid Nicola. You didn't do this.'

Morgan shakes his head sadly. 'How did you think you would get away with it Nicola?'

David looks at his father with bewilderment. 'What the …?'

His eyes begin to blaze. I have been waiting for this moment, the spring gathering inside, coiling as it always does before the attack. Out of the corner of my eye I see Art rising from the chair.

'You're full of shit.'

His boy's face is visibly melting before us, the features churning under the colourless skin, the beautiful mouth pulled back into a sickened grimace. He faces his father with his chin held high, his look burning into the smaller man.

'I'm sorry David.'

David lunges past the table, but Art is already between them, his small but powerful frame gripping the younger man's arms tightly as he swears and struggles.

'That's why she was at the river,' his father explains. He's watching his son without expression.

Then he adds quietly, but with cruel simplicity, 'She was there to murder her child.'

There is no victory in his voice, no acknowledgement that he has finally caught me out. There can be no triumph with this appalling find before him and the sight of David breaking up before his eyes. Instead his voice conveys a deep sorrow, a frightening lack of hope. It is the voice of a totally defeated man.

He'd had the choice. He could have told David his doubts about me and perhaps his son would have taken notice in time. Instead he'd preferred to guard their newfound relationship rather than rock the boat any further. Now his defeat is so great, his pity for David so deep, that he cannot even feel anger. I see no venom rising in his expression, now turned toward me, and I know that with typical Morgan thinking the same emotions he bears towards Kyle McLaughlin are at play towards me: what is done is done. There are to be no excuses, no recriminations. There is only the bare fact of fact.

He walks around the struggling body of his son and comes to a halt in front of me, his back turned to the corpse. He looks at me over his glasses. 'Didn't you consider adoption? Plenty of people would have had him. Whoever he was.'

'For *fuck's sake* Nicola, will you please tell them?' Gasping from the effort to escape Art, David stands still now, but his eyes, golden under the strip light, beseech me to wipe away Morgan's words.

I raise my head, shrug and turn away from him.

'His name was Joseph.' I say.

David's face is frozen with the horror of hearing a revelation beyond comprehension and, more fatally, beyond redemption. He shakes himself, face clouding with disbelief. 'Oh come on ....'

192

'Joseph.' I repeat.

His bottom lip begins to quiver. He is quite still now, his eyes wide and staring. He takes a step toward me but Art's fingers, still tight on his arms, clench like pinions.

'Why?'

He searches my face wildly. Finding no answer, he swings round to face his father. 'You knew about all this? You knew about it and you didn't tell me?'

Morgan shakes his head.

'I didn't know about him,' he points at the table. 'I had no idea. I was just suspicious of her. It's not surprising really, is it?'

'And you didn't tell me?'

'David, for God's sake. She tells us nothing about her past. She makes no secret that there's a secret. It was more for you than me to question that. It was none of my business, was it?' He sighs. 'I was going to talk to you – something James said. Years ago he knew her from Salisbury. I was going to tell you about that but then she got pregnant.'

Immediately David's face drains of colour. He turns and stares with an empty expression, first at my face, then at my stomach. 'Oh my God.' He steps towards me. 'Our baby ....'

I make no reply.

He begins to tremble, his mouth stretching and quivering. He pushes a hand through his hair, leaving it poised in mid air, as if stunned, his gaze dropping momentarily as if it can wipe away his torment. Then he looks at me, his eyes cold and focussed. 'What will you do to that?' he says menacingly. 'Will you chuck that in the river? Will you kill that too?'

I look up and meet his eye. 'No, David. There is no reason for your child to die.'

For a second he's suspended in disbelief. He goes to hit me but the arm pauses in mid-air, as if something inside him has clutched it. He presses his head deep into his hands and a terrible sound comes from his body. It is not a cry or a scream, but a wracking escape of breath which catches in his throat, a drawn-out, hysterical warbling.

'David,' his father pleads, his face clouding with fear.

But David doesn't hear him. He looks demented, pressing his fingers into his mouth, his eyes staring blankly at the wall in front of him.

For a moment there is silence, then it's followed by a choking indrawn breath that sounds as if it has pierced his throat and reached his heart. He's being strangled by grief. Tears course down his face and spit hangs in a fine web, stretching from his mouth to his fingers.

Morgan takes hold of his shoulders but the younger man pulls away, staring at the saliva with a morbid, almost childish curiosity. He trembles slightly and stares up at me with a sudden lucidity, searching my face.

'Oh Nicky. Why?'

'David, please,' I say quietly, 'this is nothing towards you. This is nothing to do with us.'

'No, no.'

'Please, listen.'

'Why?'

'David I ....'

'Oh God!' David sinks to his knees, his fingers stretching out into the air, his eyes seeking blindly. He rocks back and forward on the floor, his head cradled deep in his arms. 'Oh God! Oh God!'

Morgan steps towards him and a single tear weaves down his cheek. He extends a hand towards his son's shoulder.

My body jumps as David swings round and strikes out savagely. He catches Morgan with the back of his hand, in the stomach, winding him. 'Get off me! Don't you ever touch me again. Don't any of you ever touch me again.'

He straightens and shoots a madman's look around at the three of us, his mouth open and his eyes rolling. His breath rasps in his throat. 'Don't touch me,' he says a third time.

'David ....'

He turns to me. 'You shut up.'

'It's not ....'

He shakes his head wildly. 'You shut up you murdering cow. You filthy, lying, fucking *bitch*.'

But he takes a step backward as he says it, as if one part of him is still loath to cause me actual physical harm. Froth forms white flecks on his quivering lips and his eyes have glazed over. Inside a voice warns me I should stay back, that he's not in control. But the other side, which thinks I can always control him, control him no matter what, steps forward of its own accord.

'"A disgusted wisdom ....",' I say quietly. '"... all the dark voices that in secrecy are found.".' Wasn't that what you wrote David? Wasn't that what you wanted?'

But he ignores the question. Instead he mutters,

'I should have known. That sound at the river – it was a child screaming.'

'I love you.'

He goes for me – and I see the blow before I feel it, before Art can reach him. His fist shoots out of the air like a bullet and I am aware of my body crumpling.

The wind rushes against the window one more time and once more I hear that strange, desolate whistling, the lonely cry of the unborn. Then it recedes as quickly as it came – and all is silent.

Chapter Twenty Three

As usual you foresaw all. Your nails on my wrist you flung me in the corner – and kicked it out of sight.

You stood with a coldness in your eye, clothed in your expensive new suit, staring with distaste at my discount-store dress, my little worn-out shoes. There was silence then, though you continued to speak, my head filled with visions of how you entered my life, filling that basic need.

And after you'd finished your charming little piece, I saw how good you'd got, no need for the little blonde down the lane no more and I said – 'What am I supposed to do now?' and you snapped, 'Apologise to your father.'

'From the devil to the deep blue sea,' I said. 'From the frying pan to the fire. Besides, you think he would forgive me for this?'

'Do what you like,' you laughed. 'It's your mess.'

Then you moved towards me, (crouched in the corner of the room,) your shadow, like a fist – and I remembered that first time, sitting on the bus, you leaned over to me with your syrup breath and you said,

'I would give a million pounds – for a smile on that pretty face.'

I was eighteen, bright and daisy-fresh, and I turned to look at your lush eyes and already I felt it coming like the spring, light slipping through the darkness of my life, and later that day, with a smile on my face, I thought of my father pacing the house.

'You loved me,' I said, crouching between you and the sick door of the sick, sick, room and you didn't fight, you just pinched my cheek and you said that some were suckers for getting hurt.

'It's not just me who's going to get hurt.' That was the first time I touched you, you were angry, your mouth twisting and you said, with your hands in my hair, your breath on my face,

rammed against the wall … you said, 'You can't stop me Nicola, you know what I'm like when I want something … You know what I am and you know you can't touch me.'

'I can touch you both,' I replied, and you just laughed – 'Oh yes, the river woman, weaving and meandering around other peoples' lives ….'

'I've heard,' I said, laughing as your face turned to fire, 'I've heard that she's not so sure ….'

Then your hands are round my throat, my head smashed against the door, blood on a linoleum floor. Then your fist, coming out of nowhere, your final words: 'You bitch! You're lucky I don't kill you, you fucking little whore.'

And then (lying on the floor) you leave, the short clunk-click of the belt, cutting the chaff from the wheat.

Chapter Twenty Four

I wake to Morgan murmuring my name. His voice sounds muddled, slightly dreamy. I fight a wave of nausea. Opening my eyes, I see Morgan's face through a haze of swirling objects.

'David?'

'He's gone.'

I pull myself into a sitting position. 'How long have I been out?'

'Not long. A few minutes.'

I look up at Morgan's face and am surprised to find it kind. Gently, he takes my elbow and pulls me up onto shaking feet.

'My head hurts.'

'I'm not surprised, he caught you a good one.'

'Where's he gone?'

'I don't know. Art's looking for him. Sit down Nicola – here, in this chair.'

I fall back gratefully. Before me lies the child, his face silver under the glare of the striplight. Morgan lights a cigarette and waits.

'Did you call the police?'

'Not yet. I haven't thought that far ahead.'

'Poor David.'

'Yes.'

My sight begins to clear though my head feels like someone has stuck a pickaxe into the back of it. Morgan is standing against the dresser. He takes a slow puff on the cigarette and watches me.

'Why aren't you angry?' I ask.

He sighs. 'Something like this. A mother killing her child. It doesn't deserve anger. It's too tragic for that.'

I finger the edges of the blanket. 'I had the right you know,' I say softly. 'He was my son and I had to protect him.'

Morgan steps forward and sits down opposite me. He looks at me over his glasses. 'You had the right in your own head. A court won't see it like that Nicola. And David won't see it like that.'

I shake my head. 'I don't care. They can't take away that choice. I didn't want him to live. I didn't want to live. We were *both* supposed to die, don't you understand, it wasn't just him.'

'But you changed your mind.'

I look across at the young plants I have placed on the windowsill and lovingly cared for, prayer plants. I chose them because David told me they were his mother's favourite.

'Because it wasn't enough.'

He looks at me strangely. 'What do you mean, "it wasn't enough"? Enough of what?'

I don't answer him. Outside those church bells are ringing again. I turn my head and look around the kitchen, absorbing the neat dresser, the cups and plates piled high in the sink from our rush to get ready for the exhibition, the cold brick floor, the little windows with their crumbling paint. Then I look at the child, lying on the table before me: the pale features, the little mouth, the outstretched hands.

I turn my face to the strip light. 'Can you turn that off please – put the other one on?'

He looks surprised, then nods. Putting down the cigarette, he turns on the small lamp first and moves to the wall switch. I thank him. 'Sorry – it was driving me mad. Could I have a cigarette please?'

He's never seen me smoke. I light it and inhale deeply.

'I thought I'd use the opportunity to give up. Never works though does it? Once a smoke always a smoker.'

'It was a good try.'

'It's like the saplings,' I say quietly.

'What?'

'The saplings. Those baby trees they put in to replace the ones they've destroyed. They don't look the same, do they?'

Morgan looks at me curiously.

'Do they?'

He smiles slightly. 'No, I don't suppose they do.'

'It's what I hate about us humans. We think we can trick everything. We think we can replace everything we've taken away. I hate those little trees with their plastic ties, all in their neat little lines. Why can't they scatter them a bit – at least try to make them look a bit natural?'

Morgan's face has gone blank. I look at him sadly.

'We were finished, don't you understand? Me and him. There was nothing left. But it was the questions. I couldn't die while there were still questions. Everything he said, everything he promised.'

'What are you talking about Nicola – questions about what?'

I shake my head. 'It doesn't matter. You'll know soon enough. Tell David, please, tell him I said it – he'll remember. I never imagined what happened between us would happen. I didn't plan it. I warned him, I told him it was a gamble. It's all risk isn't it – a game of chance?' I look into Morgan's eyes. 'But you can't replace, you can't ever heal. Don't you understand? That's what he tried to do. That's what we all tried to do.'

'Try to heal?' Morgan mutters, slightly incredulous. 'Your child was in the river.'

'My child has been saved.'

Morgan looks at me oddly and turns his head as if listening to the wind which hurries around the house, its fingers pushing into the gutters and winding their way under tiles. I feel, suddenly, as if all my time at Morton Farm has been this way, the reproachful sky, the unusual, battering storms. Then the early summer, the lack of rain, the shallow Dale. This moment of discovery has been contrived against me, the seasons turning prematurely, the soul of the river screaming.

There is the sound of a car coming up the drive followed by a screech of brakes.

'Art,' Morgan says quietly. The car door slams and there is an urgent pounding of feet on the driveway.

Art throws open the door. 'Call an ambulance!'

He shoots past Morgan toward the phone. Morgan rises to his feet. 'What's happened?'

''Ee's cut 'imself – smashed a bottle – covered in blood ....'

I let my head fall forward and take a deep breath.

Morgan's face turns white. 'Where is he?'

Art is moving towards the front room. 'Up in the barn,' the farmhand shouts over his shoulder, 'I'll drive you there, 'ang on.'

But Morgan, without a glance in my direction, snatches up his bag and is gone, his footsteps racing urgently down the drive.

I listen as Art shouts directions into the telephone. Then he rushes back into the kitchen and swings round wildly looking for Morgan.

'He went to David,' I say quietly.

He gives me one final, terrible glare: every dislike, every contempt he has ever felt for me is there in his fish eyes. Then he too turns and leaves with the same urgency which brought him. I listen to the sound of the departing van without moving, my finger still stroking the edge of the blanket.

I am alone.

The minutes tick by. I stare out of the window but there is only darkness. From somewhere I think I can hear the gentle flow of the river, the endless churning of stone and silt. I can picture my face, blue with cold, reflected in the swollen waters

201

like a Narcissus in reverse. I tremble at the memory of such self-loathing. And at the same time the cold truth of the stone cutting under my legs, my numb fingers. It took more strength than I'd thought possible.

I sigh, forcing the memory away. On the table, next to the dead child, sits the bottle of champagne. I reach out and turn it round to read the label. It's expensive, the best. I put it back down. Walking over to the window, I can already hear the siren wailing over the hill and see the ambulance's blue light coming to a halt outside the barns. Someone must have waited on the drive, I think, to show them where he is. I stand for many minutes, craning my head at the window, until the siren wails into the night for a second time and the blue light makes its way back toward Morton.

Turning to the dresser, I open the left-hand drawer. The scissors are there. Silver, dress-making ones, another remnant from the days of May Morgan. I lift them and approach the table.

'They will know your name,' I say. I stroke the top of the child's head softly before stretching out a hand and gingerly lifting the edge of the green sleeve, where I know it is. The scissors are sharp, they snip easily and it is in my hand. The little white hospital tag, chafed and filthy, and the faded words:

Joseph McLaughlin

I turn away and sigh.

The house is silent, slightly eerie. I walk into the utility room and take Morgan's Barbour down from its peg, placing the tag carefully its pocket. Now that I have my answers, I will not return to the Dale because the sunshine has stolen the water.

But there are other places where the river swells, the Bristol Estuary for instance. And it will speed up the journey, I think, if I hitchhike there in a low-cut dress. There is no need to change.